Jared w

Shannon to...
ran to the door. The dogs whined and pranced in
anticipation and she knew exactly how they felt.
Her heart was racing like a bullet train.

The door to his truck slammed shut, and she
heard his footsteps on the porch. He unlocked
the door and stepped inside, carrying his duffel
bag under one arm. His uniform was dusty and
dirty. He looked exhausted. And as sexy as hell.
"I...waited...."

"You didn't have to, but I'm glad you did."

Suddenly Shannon couldn't stand being so far
from him. It was almost as if she had to make
sure he was real. She crossed to him. "Are
you...are you all right?"

"For the most part. I'm dead tired, starved and
filthy, but other than that—"

"Thank God," she whispered, her eyes filling with
tears. Without thinking of the consequences, she
put her arms around him and laid her head on his
chest.

Jared's duffel bag hit the floor with a thump.
And then he kissed her with incredible heat
and passion....

Dear Reader,

I've always enjoyed mail-order-bride stories, so when the opportunity presented itself to give men equal time, so to speak, I was intrigued. And a Texas man at that, sworn to uphold the law at a lonely outpost. I simply couldn't resist.

Being a Texan, there's a remote possibility I might be prejudiced, but I do believe the men in my state have a special larger-than-life quality, and my hero, Jared Markham, is no exception. He's just about the kindest, bravest man a woman could ask for—a real modern-day Lancelot. So, when Shannon Kramer goes looking for a place to hide and a man to protect her, Jared fills all her requirements and then some.

I hope after reading *Some Kind Of Hero* you'll agree with me that if the magazine *Texas Men* was available, Jared would have made the cover.

Happy Reading,

Sandy Steen

Sandy Steen
SOME KIND OF HERO

Harlequin Books

TORONTO • NEW YORK • LONDON
AMSTERDAM • PARIS • SYDNEY • HAMBURG
STOCKHOLM • ATHENS • TOKYO • MILAN
MADRID • WARSAW • BUDAPEST • AUCKLAND

For Dodie,
Who shows me every day what real heroism is.

ISBN 0-373-25712-0

SOME KIND OF HERO

Copyright © 1996 by Sandy Steen.

Prologue

"WHAT YOU NEED is a woman," Wynette Dickerson informed her friend, and part-time employer. "Correction. What you need is a wife."

Jared Markham didn't even look up from strapping on the standard issue holster and Glock 40, now riding comfortably on his right hip. "If you're going to start in about that magazine again, forget it. Even if I did need a woman, I sure wouldn't go looking for one in the want ads."

"It's not the want ads." Wynette, a friend, the waitress at the Pecos Café in Alpine, and the woman who had washed and cleaned once a week for Jared since his wife had died two years earlier, propped a hand on her bony hip. "And before you get your back up, there's absolutely nothin' wrong with puttin' an ad in one of these." She held out a copy of *Texas Men* magazine. "Why, my cousin Lerlene's friend answered a personal ad in the *Alaska Men* magazine, and first thing you know, she was off to Anchorage to get hitched."

"I'm happy for her, but that doesn't mean—"

"This," she waved the magazine in the air, "is a bona fide publication. On the up and up. Strictly legit. And if you ask me—"

"I didn't."

"Now, there you go. That's exactly your problem. You never speak up for yourself. Not about somethin' personal anyway. You've kept to yourself too long. You need the comfort and softness a woman—a good woman—can offer, and as far as I can see, you're either too shy or too stubborn to go find one on your own."

Jared adjusted the holster, and the leather creaked as if in protest to the unnecessary handling. The truth was, he did need a woman.

And the admission swamped him with guilt.

How could he even think about another woman when Amy had been gone barely two years? Two lonely, desolate years. Two years of feeling as if his empty, barren soul would never again be nourished by love. How could he even contemplate the idea of marriage, much less the actuality?

But the fact was, he *had* been contemplating the idea of marriage. Actually wrestling with the idea was more appropriate. Ever since the incident on Santiago Peak.

"You haven't been the same since they hauled you down off that mountain." When he glanced at Wynette, she shook her finger at him. "And don't you try to deny it."

"I'm not denying anything." Jared headed for the front of the Victorian style house and the small parlor he had converted into an office. Wynette followed, stopping in the doorway.

"How long has it been since that business on Santiago Peak?" she asked, leaning against the doorframe. "A week? Two weeks?"

"Fifteen days."

"And you been walkin' around here with a hangdog look on your face ever since. I know you think I'm a real buttinsky, but I just wanna see you happy."

"Plastering my private life all over the pages of a damned magazine won't make me happy," he snapped.

There was a long pause, before Wynette replied, "Well, excuse me, I was just tryin' to help. You don't have to bite my head off." Then she pushed away from the door and left.

Jared sighed, knowing he had been a real jerk. Wynette was a good friend and didn't deserve his foul mood. A mood that basically stemmed from the fact that she was right. He hadn't been the same since the incident. The fact that even now he preferred to think of what happened as an incident rather than an accident was an indication of his denial. Probably because the word *accident* implied the unexpected, a mishap, something he had no control over.

The lack of control, the pure happenstance of the situation, was what had finally made him see himself, and his life in the harsh light of reality. So much of the time that had passed since Amy's death scarcely caused a ripple in his memory, yet he remembered that night on Santiago Peak with startling clarity.

He had gone into the foothills of the Del Norte Mountains after some hunters who'd been illegally tracking desert bighorn sheep. The hunters had eluded him, slithering over the unforgiving terrain in the darkness like invisible snakes. Frustrated at having lost his quarry, he had started back toward his truck, mumbling some uncomplimentary words for the hunters . . . and not paying attention to where he was walking. The toe of his boot caught on a length of exposed root, and he went ass-end over teakettle down fifty yards of mountainside. A rookie, tenderfoot kind of thing to do.

Reacting instinctively as he tumbled, he had made a desperate grab at a huge boulder hoping to stop his bone-jarring descent. But for the second time that night his judgment was bad. The slab of rock wasn't firmly embedded in the ground. As he grabbed hold, it gave way and brought a rock slide with it.

The boulder literally chased him down the hill. Half rolling, half sliding, he came to an abrupt stop when his body slammed into a rocky outcropping at the bottom of the hill. The sixty-pound-plus boulder come to an abrupt stop against his left foot.

Because he had landed facedown and at an awkward angle, he had lain trapped for three hours before Tucker Weiss, the second game warden assigned to Brewster County, had found him. Thanks to sturdy

boots, he had emerged from the accident basically un-
scathed with the exception of a badly bruised ankle.
Physically he was okay. But something emotional—
maybe even spiritual—had happened to him while he
lay on that dark mountainside. For the first time in two
years he had come face-to-face with his loneliness.

The reality that he had no one.

His parents were dead. His only brother lived in
Wyoming, and years passed between their visits. His
friends, mostly other game wardens he had befriended
over his eight-year career, were scattered across the
state.

No one was waiting for him to come home.

If he had lain on that mountain for three days instead of three hours, no one would have been worried.
And if he had died...

Yes, there would have been some who grieved, but
his passing wouldn't have left an empty place in anyone's life.

The reality of his aloneness had been a cold, horrifying shock. He could still remember the fear clutching
at his heart, so powerful he felt as if he couldn't breathe.
Lying there in the darkness that fear, once recognized,
had crystallized. He loved his work, and he was proud
to be a game warden, but he didn't want to end up with
nothing to show for his life but a bunch of fellow officers standing around his casket talking about what a
great guy he had been. Until that night, Jared hadn't
realized just how much he had isolated himself since

Amy's death, how much he had truly missed sharing his life with a woman.

Strangely enough, it wasn't the major things that he missed. It was the thousand and one little intimacies that he remembered about sharing his life with Amy. The moments when he would hear her softly humming in another room, or the way she used to touch his cheek once in a while. That last moment right before she drifted off to sleep and whispered, "Sweet dreams," or the first moment she opened her eyes to a new day, smiling, eager to kiss him good morning. Her gentle manner that never failed to soothe him. She was his anchor, the calm at the center of any storm life threw his way.

As he waited to be rescued, knowing he wasn't in life-threatening danger, Jared realized that he had sealed his pain inside of himself like some kind of morbid shrine to his late wife. A painful, private shrine where only he could worship. He had sealed himself off from life. And in doing so, he realized that his heart had become as isolated as the part of Texas he was sworn to protect.

In his job, good instincts could mean the difference between life and death. And that night, every instinct he had was telling him that he *had* to change his life.

Even now, days afterward, he was still struggling with knowing change was necessary, yet not knowing how to accomplish it.

With a weary sigh he raked his hands through his thick blond hair, then went to find Wynette and offer his most sincere apology. Hell, maybe she was even right about that magazine. That admission in itself proved how desperate he was. Still, even though it was certainly an unorthodox method of starting a relationship, the more he thought about it, the more he realized it might be his only realistic approach. After all, it would solve his main problem. Namely, that there weren't many women in the sparsely populated Big Bend area, and he had precious little time to go courting.

What could it hurt? Besides, Jared thought, as he headed to the kitchen to find Wynette, he probably wouldn't get more than a handful of responses anyway. What were the chances of finding the kind of woman he could spend the rest of his life with—a million to one?

1

GAZING OUT THE BIG bay window in his kitchen, Jared watched the early morning sun spill over the Glass Mountains, and wondered if the isolation of his job had finally affected his mind. Change, and a need to end the loneliness was one thing, but what he had done was beginning to feel more like insanity.

Advertising for a wife.

What kind of man gets a wife from a want ad? And what kind of woman answers such an ad?

At least he hadn't come off sounding like a complete jerk in the magazine, and it had painted a picture of him as a man of old-fashioned, but not outdated values, strong morals and a deep and abiding respect for women. And it stated the most important traits for the relationship he was contemplating—honesty and self-reliance. Any woman answering his ad knew where he stood, and what he was looking for.

Raising a cup of steaming black coffee to his lips, he glanced at the old metal milk carrier on his kitchen table, stuffed to the brim with responses to his ad. Over a hundred letters from women looking for...for what? Love, security, steady sex? Jared had read them all, and had been amazed, even shocked to discover that there were so many women anxious to jump into a relationship, sight unseen. And downright stunned to discover many of them spoke freely of their need for a physical relationship. Very physical.

At age thirty-one, women's lib and the sexual revolution weren't exactly foreign concepts, but he had to admit he had been totally unprepared for the candor and borderline pornographic explicitness some of the women had expressed in outlining their likes and dislikes. One thing was for sure. After wading through his mountain of correspondence, he knew he had been out of the dating loop too long to ever be glib and charming, or any of the other things these women seemed to want.

Out of all the letters, he had found only three that sounded even remotely as if they'd been written by someone he might be interested in. Now all he had to do was call the women, and possibly arrange a meeting. Yeah, that's all he had to do.

Jared set his coffee cup on the counter and reached for the phone, then stopped.

He couldn't do this.

It just wasn't his nature to call up some strange woman and make small talk, then ask her if she wanted to come size him up while he was doing the same to her. He just couldn't do it.

Once again he gazed out the window at the mountains, watching the last traces of the night's purple shadows fading before the sun. They looked so majestic, so strong. He had always found great solace in their beauty, great strength in their majesty. And though he considered them as no less powerful, since the incident at Santiago Peak he had seen them in a different light. For perhaps the first time in his life, Jared had identified with their solitude. He was a solitary creature in need of warmth, companionship. He didn't want to stand alone against time like a mountain.

So what were his alternatives? The sameness he had grown pitifully comfortable with since Amy died. A lonely sameness. That wasn't an alternative. It was a death sentence.

No, he *had* to do this. He had to pick up the phone and call these women. He had come this far. Losing his nerve now was silly.

"No guts, no glory," he mumbled, jerking up the receiver. His hand shook as he dialed the first number.

Forty-five minutes later, Jared hung up from his second call. So far he was batting zero.

The first woman, a twenty-nine-year-old dental hygienist from San Angelo, had been appalled at the description of how remote his home was, and how self-sufficient she would have to be.

"You mean you really don't go into town except for once a week?" she had asked. Followed shortly by, "Do you mean it's literally forty miles to the nearest restaurant? What do you do for entertainment?"

The second candidate wasn't much more receptive. The thirty-five-year-old divorcée with a soft southern accent had asked, "You mean you actually go around hunting poachers? With a gun? How could you do that?"

The thought of a third rejection was enough to make him give up on the whole idea. But, he had come this far, and there was only one candidate left.

"What the hell," he said, dialing the number.

STANDING BESIDE THE pay phone in the hallway outside her rented room, Shannon Kramer stared at the number scribbled on the piece of paper her landlady had just handed her. The piece of paper that might be her ticket to eventual freedom, or back to an intolerable existence. It was a risk. Maybe this was the man in the ad, or maybe it was a trap set by her ex-husband.

If only she wasn't so desperate. If only she could have come up with any other way to keep herself and her daughter out of danger. God knows she had tried everything she could think of: changing names, hair color—hers, and Lily's—padding to make herself look pounds heavier than her usual willowy build, even dressing herself and her daughter up as males. None of it had worked.

Hal always found them.

Her ex-husband's network of survivalist good old boys worked like a trap where she and Lily were concerned. They were everywhere. It was almost as if he had his own personal army of spies. Whenever, wher-

ever she and Lily surfaced, eventually they were spotted, and the news got back to Hal.

And the last time he tracked them down, he had almost strangled her to death when she refused to tell him
where she had hidden his daughter. He would have
succeeded if her burly ex-bouncer landlord hadn't arrived, and taken a hand. He did succeed in issuing a
threat. While the landlord kept him pinned to a wall
awaiting the police, Hal had vowed he would hunt her
down. There was no place she could hide, he promised. No person she could trust. He told her that she and
Lily belonged to him like everything else he owned, and
if he couldn't have them, no one would.

Shannon could remember that horrifying, bone-
chilling moment as though it were five minutes ago instead of five months. There had been so much venom
in his voice. So much hate. She never doubted for an
instant that he meant every word. She hadn't waited to
press charges. Instead she and Lily had gone as far un-
derground as they could. But it wasn't far enough. She
had begun to think it would never be far enough.

Then fate had intervened, or maybe one of her many
prayers had been answered. Either way, the day she had
happened across a copy of *Texas Men* magazine, and
Jared Markham's ad while waiting in a bus station, she
had decided he was exactly what she needed. His home
was remote, he made infrequent trips into the city, and
his job required him to be gone a great deal.

Money and nerves worn almost to nothing after playing Hal's freakish game of hide-and-seek for over a year and a half, Shannon had taken one look at the ad, and felt her heart leap for joy. She knew she couldn't take much more of the continual stalking. Every day, every hour was an eternity spent looking over her shoulder, scrutinizing every stranger. She was constantly on guard, jumping at shadows while trying to pretend to Lily that she had everything under control. That everything was going to be just fine.

Who was she kidding? Nothing would ever be fine again until Hal gave up on them. And she knew that would never happen. Hal was as desperate to find her as she was to stay out of his grasp.

So, she had no choice. Either this man, this Jared Markham was the real McCoy or he wasn't. If he wasn't, she and Lily would continue running. Shannon dialed the number.

THE PHONE was picked up on the first ring. "Markham."

"Hello," Shannon said nervously. "Could I speak with Jared—"

"Jared Markham. Yes, I'm, uh, Jared Markham," the man said. He sounded as nervous as she was. "Is this Shannon Kramer?"

Despite the fact that Shannon had written the letter in good faith, she figured the odds were at least a thousand to one that he would contact her. Now that her plan had suddenly gone from concept to reality, her heart rate jumped and her nerves tingled partly from excitement, partly from fear.

"Hello," Jared said again. "Are you still there?"

"Yes, I'm . . . I'm here." She licked her dry lips, and knew a sudden, intense craving for a cigarette, despite the fact that she had abandoned the habit almost six years ago.

"I have the right Shannon Kramer, don't I? You answered an ad in *Texas Men* magazine?"

"That's me. I mean, yes. You've got the right Shannon Kramer." She reminded herself that he was several hundred miles away, and no threat. She reminded herself that he was, in fact, her rescue plan, and possibly her last hope. She couldn't afford to make any mistakes now.

"I, uh, just want you to know that I've never done this before," he sort of blurted out after a long pause. "Put an ad in a magazine, I mean. I'm kind of nervous."

"Then that makes us even because I've never answered one before. And I'm . . . I'm nervous, too."

But Shannon's nervousness had little to do with first-date jitters. Her nerves were taut with months of looking over her shoulders. Jared Markham might very well be the solution to her problems, but she had to be sure. Since her recent past had taught her the best way to deal with difficulty was to meet it head-on, she jumped in with her first question.

"The article didn't mention whether or not you had ever been married. Do you mind if I ask?"

"My . . . my wife died two years ago."

"Oh. I'm so sorry, Jared."

It was the first time she called him by his name, and for a reason he couldn't explain, the sound of it poured over him like sunshine on the first day of spring. How long had it been since he had heard caring in a woman's voice? And her sympathy was real. That was in her voice, too. If this woman was one tenth what her voice promised, he owed Wynette a big apology for ever doubting her advice.

"Thanks," he said.

"You didn't say anything about it in the ad, so I, uh, take it there were no children."

Jared's breath hit the back of his throat, and his fingers tightened on the receiver. Pain, sharp and familiar, hit him like a fist to his gut. For a moment, her seemingly innocent question tilted his world, spinning him back into painful memories.

"Jared?"

"No," he said finally. "No children."

"But you like them? Kids, I mean."

"Like them?" God, she didn't know what she was asking. He loved kids. He and Amy had planned on having a houseful. "Y-yes."

"Good," she said softly.

Jared was struggling so hard to keep the memories at bay that her response didn't register. "I, uh, I'd really like to meet you," he said, wanting to steer the conversation away from children.

"Yes. I'm anxious to meet you, too."

When Jared hung up a few moments later, he stared at the phone, a little stunned at what had transpired. And how quickly. Once they started making plans to meet, everything just sort of snowballed. She told him that she had some vacation time coming, and before he realized it they had made plans to meet this Sunday afternoon.

He had offered to pay Shannon's airfare from Austin to San Angelo, the nearest airport, but she had declined, saying that she didn't think they should start off owing each other anything but an open mind, and a positive attitude. He thought it strange that she opted to travel by bus, considering her eagerness to arrange an almost immediate meeting, but then he decided that maybe she hated to fly.

It dawned on him that more than anything he had based his opinion of Shannon Kramer on the honesty and credibility he heard in her voice. And his own instincts. It also dawned on him that she had asked most of the questions, ending the conversation with more knowledge of him than he had about her. He hadn't asked if she had ever been married, or what her background was, or . . . anything. In a matter of minutes he had committed himself to meeting a woman he had never seen, with a possible result of matrimony. He had never done anything so . . . so spontaneous, or risky, in his life. Suddenly panicked, Jared reached for the phone, intending to call her back and call the whole thing off, but he stopped.

Or rather, remembering the sound of her voice stopped him. She sounded so...warm. And he needed warmth.

No, he cautioned himself. This wasn't about warmth. This was about his need for companionship. He couldn't—wouldn't—allow himself to think about warmth. Even thinking about it felt disloyal to Amy's memory.

He had loved, and been loved, deeply and passionately. Love like that only came along once in a lifetime. Shannon Kramer might be the answer to his loneliness but he didn't expect to love her. Not the way he had loved Amy.

JARED MARKHAM might be the answer to Shannon's prayers, but that didn't make lying to him any easier. In fact, if anything, it made it harder. He sounded so solid, so reliable. And self-confident. Exactly the kind of man she needed.

The twist to this truly bizarre situation was that Jared sounded like the kind of man she'd want to marry. A man she could depend on. A man that was secure enough in himself to give his wife love *and* support. To be a true partner in every sense of the word. For a fleeting moment she allowed herself to fantasize about a real relationship. What would it be like to love Jared? To make love to him?

Oh, this was crazy. She couldn't afford daydreams. And even if Jared turned out to be the man of her dreams, she fell one mark shy of his criteria. Honesty. For there to be even a faint hope of her dreams becoming reality she would have to be totally honest with him. And she couldn't do that.

Sometimes when she thought of everything that had happened and how Hal had driven her to her current state of desperation, she wondered how she could have ever cared about him. But she had, in the beginning anyway.

Growing up as the middle child and only girl in a family of eight, Shannon had learned to stand on her own two feet at an early age. Her independence and self-confidence had been forged in a fire of teasing and torment by her brothers, and she had emerged tempered and flexible, able to take whatever life dealt her. By the time she was in junior high school, she could keep a house, sew and care for her younger brothers every bit as well as her mother. And her skills were put to the test because that was the year her mother became sick. From then until the time Alice Kramer died three years later, for all intents and purposes, Shannon became a mother. Her father did what he could to help, but working two jobs to support his family left him precious little time for parenting. Most of the responsibility fell squarely on Shannon's shoulders.

Dreaming of a better life for herself, she worked nights at the local movie theater to earn her tuition at a community college.

And then came Hal Jackson.

He was good-looking, and treated her as if she were as delicate as English bone china. He made her laugh, and taught her how to have fun. With Hal she felt special and treasured. He offered his protection, and painted a picture of the wonderful life they would have together. For the first time in her life Shannon let someone look after her.

But it didn't take long after they were married for her to realize that Hal's idea of love was one-sided. His side. And his idea of protection was to isolate her from everyone but himself. She had already begun to entertain thoughts of leaving him when she learned she was pregnant. Never one to give up when the going got tough, she stayed, and tried to make the best of her marriage, but when Lily was born Hal got worse, not better. His behavior became obsessive, and the only time he spent away from her was when he went out with his gun-club friends, and an occasional weekend of survival training.

Then the abuse began. Mostly verbal slurs with an occasional slap or shove, but Shannon knew she had to get away from him. Twice she tried, and twice Hal brought her back. Lily was three by the time she was finally able to find sanctuary in a women's shelter, and file for divorce. Fool that she was, she thought that would be the end of it. But it was only the beginning.

Hal's obsessive behavior escalated. He harassed her constantly, causing her to lose first one job then another. Despite a court order, he showed up on her doorstep whenever he chose. Shannon called the police, talked to her lawyer, the judge, anybody who would listen, but to no avail. Later she learned that the judge, district attorney and several police officers were among Hal's gun-club buddies. In this case, camaraderie bred contempt—for her. Soon, it became clear that the deck was stacked against her, and that her only hope was to get as far away from Hal as she could. So, she and Lily had left in the middle of the night with only one suitcase each and the few dollars Shannon had been able to save. But they couldn't keep running forever. She was desperate to throw Hal off their scent.

And desperate women do desperate things. Answering the ad was the biggest risk she'd ever taken, but in hindsight it just might pay off.

Unfortunately, making it to Alpine didn't mean she and Lily were home free. Once she got there, the desperation would require more half truths, and outright lies. And for a woman who prided herself on honesty, deception—no matter how justifiable—was a bitter pill to swallow. But she would swallow it. Of course she would. Because she had to. Because she had run out of options, places to hide, and almost run out of strength. Jared Markham was her last hope.

But she knew from experience that even last hopes should have a backup plan. They would go to Alpine, and pray that Jared accepted her. If he didn't, well . . . Frankly, Shannon had no idea what she would do next except cut her losses, and move on. She only knew that as hard as it would be, if Jared turned his back on them, she and Lily would survive. Somehow, some way.

"Mama?"

She glanced down into the bright blue eyes of her five-year-old daughter, Lily. Amazingly, Lily had blossomed once free of her father's stinging verbal abuse. Even though she had no permanent home or friends to play with, the once quiet child had come into her own. She laughed freely, and seemed to bear no severe emotional scars.

"Mama, are we gonna move again?"

Shannon bent down until she was at eye level with the one person she loved above all else. The one person she would protect with her life if need be. "Yes, sweetheart," she replied, her husky voice even huskier with emotion. "But maybe this time we can stay for a while."

"Oh, boy." Lily threw her arms around her mother's neck, and gave her a quick hug before drawing back. "I'll cross my fingers, okay, Mama. That'll help, won't it?"

"Sure."

"You, too, Mama."

"Me, too, baby." Shannon held up her right hand, fingers crossed. "Me, too."

2

SHE NEVER SHOULD have come. It was a bad idea from the beginning. Whatever possessed her to think she could look this man in the eyes and lie without him seeing her for the fool she was? She would never have considered it in a million years if she hadn't been so desperate. But absolute desperation hadn't prevented her conscience from eating away at her like acid ever since she had called Jared Markham back to tell him she would be arriving late Sunday afternoon.

And she had almost phoned him a dozen times since then to call off their meeting. But she hadn't. Every time she reached for the phone a mental image of Hal's face, twisted with rage, flashed across her mind.

Now, here she was sitting in a café across from the bus station waiting for him to arrive. Waiting to play out the scene she hoped would eventually win her a hiding place. Her strategy, if you could call it that, was simple, if slightly vague. When she met Jared she would stay as close to the truth as possible without revealing her real reason for answering his ad. Simple, but lying, even by degrees, went against every principle, every moral fiber Shannon possessed.

So she would admit to her lie of omission where Lily was concerned, and that she knew she had probably ruined any chance they might have had. He deserved the truth face-to-face. She owed him that much. With luck, she would come across as exactly what she was— a proud, but poor single mother. That is, if she got the chance, before he stormed out of the café.

"Mama, can I have another Coke?"

"It's not in the budget, sweetie. Besides, too many soft drinks aren't good for your teeth," Shannon told her daughter without taking her gaze from the front window of the café.

Jared had suggested they meet at the Pecos Café in case he got held up, or her bus got in early. The bus had arrived ahead of schedule, and Shannon was grateful for his suggestion because the café window provided her with a view of the street. And she wanted to be sure to see him before he saw her.

"Refills are free for kids under six."

Shannon looked around at the waitress, a thinnish woman with a wide smile. "Thanks, but I'd rather she have water."

"Better for her anyway. Let me top off your glass." The waitress stepped to the counter, picked up a pitcher of ice water, then stepped back, and filled the two glasses on the table. "How'd those grilled cheese sandwiches do you ladies?"

"Fine, thanks." Shannon quickly glanced out the front window again.

"You wanna order somethin' else?"

"No. I, uh . . . I'm waiting for someone, but . . ."

"Must be a man."

"What makes you say that?"

"'Cause you've just about mutilated that poor napkin."

Shannon glanced down to discover that she had picked at the paper napkin until almost half of it was in pieces on the table.

"No woman gets that worked up less she's waitin' for a man."

"I didn't realize I'd made such a mess." Shannon quickly brushed the pieces of paper into a pile, then raked them off the table into an extra napkin, and wadded it into a ball.

"Must be some guy."

"I don't know. I've never met him."

The waitress cocked her head. "You mean you're workin' yourself into a lather over a man you've never even seen?"

"And will probably never see again after today," Shannon said, her conscience taking another bite out of her confidence. "Once Jared Markham—"

"Well, I'll be. You must be Shannon Kramer."

Accustomed to denying her own name out of fear, Shannon merely looked at the woman. "I beg your pardon?"

"You are, aren't you? Jared told me you were comin' in today."

"You . . . you know him?"

"And then some. He's a regular in here. Only decent food he gets if you wanna know the truth. Listen, sugar, I'm the one that pushed him into puttin' that ad in the magazine in the first place. Like pullin' on a sat down mule, but he finally gave in. The name's Wynette Dickerson." She stuck out her hand, and Shannon shook it. "So, you're the one."

"Yes, I—I guess so."

"And who might this sweet little darlin' be?" Wynette asked, looking at Lily.

"This is my daughter, Lily. Say hello to Mrs. Dickerson."

"Hello," the child said.

"Y'all call me Wynette. Jared never told me nothin' about you havin' a kid."

Shannon glanced away. "He . . . he doesn't know."

Wynette's hazel eyes widened. "Just an oversight on your part or were you intendin' to surprise him?"

She hadn't planned on having anyone but Jared as an audience, but it couldn't be avoided. Shannon hated this. She hated the way fear now dictated her every action. This woman was an innocent bystander in her flight from cruelty, and didn't deserve to be roped into a circle of lies and a race from the devil, but for now at least, there was no other way.

Unable to look the smiling waitress in the eyes, Shannon glanced away. "I'm ashamed to admit it was deliberate. So ashamed, in fact, that I . . . I couldn't go through with this. He's probably going to hate me, but I felt the least I could do was tell him in person."

"You may have more guts than you do good sense."

"How mad is he going to be?"

"Hard to tell with Jared. He's not what you'd call real expressive."

"In this case, he's got a right to be rip-roaring mad."

"Like I said, he ain't a rip-roaring kinda guy."

"Well, at least he deserves the truth."

"How come you didn't tell him right off?"

"Uh, sweetheart," Shannon said turning to Lily. "Would you like to go over to the jukebox, and play a song?"

Lily's heart-shaped face lit up. "Can I please? Can I?"

"May I."

"May I, please, please?"

Practically before Shannon got the word *yes* out of her mouth, Lily had wiggled out of her seat, under the table, and come up on the outside of the booth.

Smiling, Shannon gave one of Lily's honey blond braids a tug. "Next time try getting out the conventional way," she said, digging in her purse for change. She handed Lily a quarter. "Pick out a good one, okay?"

"Okay," Lily said over her shoulder, already halfway to the jukebox.

When Shannon knew her daughter was out of earshot, she looked up at Wynette Dickerson. "I didn't tell him because I was afraid he wouldn't want a woman with a child." *Afraid to miss my last chance.*

"And was comin' here so important?" Wynette asked, seeming to forget her two other customers to slide into the side of the booth across from Shannon.

"Yes." That much was certainly the truth.

"Don't seem like a good way to start off, if you ask me."

"You're right, of course, but . . ."

"But?"

"I was desperate." Shannon looked the waitress in the eyes. "And tired of men thinking I'm easy because I'm alone. Tired of scratching out a living in cramped, dirty cities where people have forgotten what clean air smells like. And tired of living every minute of my life in fear of being mugged or killed, or—God forbid—of something happening to my child. I want more than that for Lily. I know that's no excuse for what I did, but when I saw Jared's ad . . ." She glanced away. "I just want a chance for us."

"You weren't born a city girl, were you?" the waitress asked. Shannon shook her head. "Figures, or you wouldn't be wantin' fresh air and space." Wynette sighed. "And what about Jared?"

"I thought maybe, just for once in my life, I'd found a trustworthy man. I should have known my luck hadn't changed."

"Had a lot of that, have you?"

"'A lot' doesn't even begin to cover it. Responsibility seems to leave a bad taste in most men's mouths. At least, the ones I've met. They're hardly interested in having children of their own, much less taking care of another man's child. I know I should have told Jared the truth, but—and this may sound corny—your friend sounded like an answer to prayer. Anyway," Shannon said, sighing deeply, "I decided to face the music. Afterward, Lily and I will move on."

"Move on? I thought you lived in San Antonio?"

"We did but . . . but I lost my job. So," she said, her voice a little too bright, her smile a little too forced, "I thought maybe we'd try California. With all those high-priced restaurants out there, there's bound to be good tips." The truth was, if her meeting with Jared turned out badly, California was as good a place as any to run.

"You wait tables?"

Shannon nodded.

In the eighteen months since her divorce from Hal, she had worked in more eateries than she cared to count. But it was an honest living, and transient, therefore convenient. There was always a diner or a café in the next town that needed another girl. And if she decided to leave on the spur of the moment, no one ever asked why.

The waitress eyed the younger woman for a second, then said, "You know, Alpine ain't exactly on the way to the coast."

"I thought it was important to set the record straight." Shannon shrugged. "Besides, one place is pretty much like the next."

"Got no folks? What about the little girl's daddy?"

"He's dead," Shannon said quickly. God forgive her, but she wished it was true. "Lily, and I are all the family we have."

Wynette frowned. "When were you planning on leavin'?"

"As . . . as soon as I talk to Jared."

"You mean today? Why, you'll be ridin' that bus all night, and for the next two days before you get to California."

"Well, I . . ." Shannon ducked her head again, then looked back at Wynette. "Actually, our ticket runs out in Phoenix."

"What are you gonna do in Phoenix?"

The tickets in her purse *did* show Phoenix as the end of the line. Not that it made much difference where they wound up if she couldn't hide out long enough for their trail to grow cold. Shannon shrugged. "The same thing I've always done. Get a job. Make a living. Keep things together as best I can. Then as soon as I manage to tuck a little cash back, we'll go on to California."

"Lord, love 'ya. You know, even though Jared ain't much of a talker, he's fair. Once he's had a chance to think about it, he may not be too upset. Sure hate to see you just tell him, then light out."

"I doubt I'll have any other choice."

"Uh, well," Wynette said, sliding out of the booth. "You're about to find out."

Shannon looked out the window to see a tall blond man in a tan-and-brown uniform across the street, headed toward the café. "Jared?"

"In the flesh," Wynette replied, then patted the young woman on the shoulder. "Good luck, sugar."

"Th-thanks." After a quick glance at Lily still enthralled with the jukebox, Shannon focused on the man striding across the two-lane street.

Huge was the only word she could think of to describe her first impression of Jared Markham. He was huge. Broad shoulders out to forever, powerful arms, and an athlete's physique. But size was definitely the dominant impression. Size, and the fact that his picture didn't do him justice. Of course, the well-fitted uniform and gun strapped to his hip added an extra dimension to his aura of power.

He looked . . . substantial. Solid and steady.

And he was handsome in the bargain. Not pretty, but virile and powerful in a way no mere good looks could claim. His blue eyes were sharp, intelligent, and his jaw looked strong enough to withstand a sledgehammer. If the words *ruggedly handsome* ever fit anyone, they fit Jared Markham.

As he stepped on the curb only a couple of yards from the café window, a boy of maybe eight or nine came racing along the sidewalk on a skateboard. Seconds away from the intersection, it was clear he would never be able to stop if he had to. Quick as a striking rattler Markham reached out, and snagged the flying youngster out of the way of possible harm.

Until that moment Shannon hadn't realized she was holding her breath in anticipation of disaster. A disaster neatly avoided by Jared Markham's instantaneous save. She half expected the tall game warden to angrily chastise the child, but to her surprise he went down on one knee, putting himself at the boy's eye level. As he pointed to the intersection then to the skateboard, she didn't have to overhear the conversation to know the finer points of sidewalk safety were being explained to the haphazard youngster. But Jared's expression was calm and concerned, firm, but gentle. Finally, he stood up, and offered his hand. The boy hesitated, obviously surprised at such a grown-up gesture, but shook the game warden's hand, then went on his way. At a much slower pace.

But what riveted Shannon was the smile on Jared Markham's face as he watched the boy move away. She got the feeling that seeing to the kid's safety was more than just a job to Jared. She got the feeling that this was a man who cared.

Swallowing the lump in her throat, Shannon realized she had just been given a glimpse of his personality that she might never have otherwise seen. A very revealing glimpse.

Until this very moment she had thought of him in the abstract, choosing not to think of him as a flesh-and-blood human being. Ashamed of her self-denial, she could no longer escape reality. Jared Markham was a real man with feelings. He was even heroic. And as she very well knew, heroes didn't grow on trees.

If she had serious reservations about how he might be with her child, they had just shrunk to mild concern. But her reservations about what she was doing, about how she was using him had just become major doubts. As much as she needed Jared, he didn't deserve to be used.

She shoved the guilty thought aside by reminding herself that she was doing this for Lily. Lily was all that mattered.

Jared gazed after the boy for several seconds, then turned and entered the café. When he stopped to give Wynette a warm greeting, she pointed to Shannon, and he looked straight at her.

As he walked toward her, Shannon's heart rate jumped, and a covey of butterflies took flight in the pit of her stomach. And when he stopped at her booth she had to clasp the hands in her lap to keep them from shaking. Torn between the desperate hope of finally being free of Hal, and the reality of what she was doing almost made her sick to her stomach.

Jared couldn't believe his eyes. This woman was beautiful. A little too pale, but maybe that was nerves. She had gorgeous green eyes, the color of the trees as evening settles on the mountainside. Her hair was dark and thick with just a hint of natural curls around her

face. Wearing very little, if any, makeup and only a
tinted lip gloss, she looked innocent and alluring at the
same time. As if she should be sitting in the middle of
a field of daisies, her lovely face lifted to the sun.

After having been thoroughly made love to only
moments before.

The thought shocked him, but not nearly so much
as the image that flashed across his mind. An image of
green eyes vibrant with desire. Of dark hair falling over
bare shoulders, bare breasts.

He hadn't expected gorgeous, but that's what she
was. And he hadn't expected his body to react so
strongly.

"Shannon?"

She offered a smile that was weak at best. "Hello."

"Have you, uh, been waiting long?"

He was so tall she had to tilt her head farther back
than usual in order to look into his face. "No, not long."

"Good." Then he took the other side of the booth,
but because of his size and build, not easily. In fact,
once he was sitting, the booth seemed to shrink.

"How was your trip?"

"Fine." Shannon chanced another quick glance at
Lily, and was relieved to see she was still occupied with
the jukebox. "Before we go any farther, I have to tell you
something."

He smiled, but it didn't quite reach his eyes. "One
look at me, and you've changed your mind?"

"No, you're fine. I mean, this is not about you or about wanting to...to get to know you." Shannon took a deep breath, gathering all her courage. She had to tell him the truth. As much as she could. And he would either forgive her, and let her and Lily stay, or he would toss her out on her rear, which, of course, he had every right to do. Shannon wondered if God heard prayers for half truths, even for a good cause.

"I wasn't completely honest when we talked on the phone."

"Oh."

"I, uh, didn't tell you that I'm divorced."

"Actually, you didn't tell me a whole lot about yourself. I take it that wasn't a memory lapse?"

Was he angry? She couldn't tell. If he was, it wasn't any brand of anger she had ever encountered. But then admittedly, she wasn't the best judge of temperaments that were less than raging. "No, it wasn't."

"Well, being divorced isn't the end of the world, nor does it earn you a scarlet letter. So, I assume there's more."

Shannon nodded. "I have a child."

Jared blinked. He wasn't sure what he had expected her to say, but announcing that she had a child was last on his list. Why would she neglect to tell him such an important fact. Unless...

"Is...is there something wrong with your child?"

"There most certainly is not." Her defense was quick, and certain. "She's a beautiful, healthy five-year-old. And very bright, I might add."

"So why keep her a secret?"

"I was going to tell you, but... Well, to be honest—"

"I wish you would."

Shannon looked into his blue eyes, and saw no forgiveness. "I had that coming."

Oh, brother, had she ever blown it.

She could see it in his eyes. Her last hope, and she'd blown it. Right now he probably wouldn't give her the time of day, much less a second chance.

She lifted her chin, refusing to look away from his gaze. All right, if she couldn't convince him to accept her then she could at least exit this disastrous situation with as much of her dignity intact as possible.

"I answered your ad because I want my child to have a real home, security. I want her to be safe and happy. I didn't tell you because I was afraid you wouldn't want a woman with a child. I've had some bad experiences in that area. My hope was that after you got to know us you would want us. Look, the fact of the matter is that I was scared. I've been on my own since Lily was a baby, and I can tell you, firsthand, that men who want what I want are few and far between."

"So, you thought a lonely widower would be an easy mark."

She tried to ignore the caustic remark but it stung. "No. Your ad sounded so . . . wonderful. The mountains, and a real home. I thought that maybe you were as lonely as I was. I thought that just maybe you needed someone as much as I do." Shannon glanced down at her hands, knotted into fists in her lap, then back up at Jared.

"Is this the part where I forgive you, and ask you to stay anyway?"

"No."

The suspicion in his eyes clearly said he didn't believe her. It was a lost cause anyway.

Shannon squared her narrow shoulders. "I wanted to apologize face-to-face because that was the least I could do after deceiving you. And yes, I *had* hoped we could work something out, but I see now that's not possible."

She had been as honest as she could be under the circumstances. As honest as she dared. From this point on, it was up to Jared Markham.

Before he could say anything, Lily came skipping up to the booth humming the tune to the popular country-and-western song she had just played on the jukebox. "Can I do it—" At her mother's raised eyebrow, she said, "May I do it again, Mama?"

"I'm sorry, baby. That was my last quarter."

The little girl's lower lip jutted out about the same time she noticed the man across from her mother.

"Lily, say hello to Mr. Markham."

The pout was forgotten as her big blue eyes trained on the stranger in the uniform. "Are you a policeman?"

For a second he frowned, and glanced away, almost as if he didn't want to look at the little girl, but it was gone so quickly Shannon wasn't sure. And a moment later he smiled at the child, and there was only kindness in his eyes.

"In a way," he said. "Only I work out in the forest and mountains instead of the city."

"But there's no bad men in the forest, only animals," Lily insisted.

"Sometimes there are bad men in the forest. Then I have to protect the animals."

His statement won instant approval with a wide smile. "I like animals." She turned to Shannon. "Don't I, Mama?" She turned back to Jared. "But I can't have a dog. We can't take a dog with us. 'Cause of all our different houses, and—"

"We've moved around a lot," Shannon interjected, hoping to sidetrack Lily.

"Uh-huh. And no dogs. That's the rule," Lily informed him, punctuating the sentence with a nod of her head. "Do you have a dog?"

"As a matter of fact, I have two."

Lily's eyes went as round as half dollars. "You got two?"

"Have," her mother corrected.

"What's their names?"

"Lily, you're pestering Mr. Markham."

"But, Mama—"

"It's okay," Jared said, gazing at Shannon over the top of Lily's head.

"She can be terribly single-minded when she wants to be. And a real question box."

"How else will she learn?"

There was a wealth of patience in his voice, and Shannon imagined him using the same gentle authoritarian tone of voice with the skateboarder earlier. Jared looked back at Lily. "One's name is Mack, and the other's name is Pit."

Lily wrinkled her nose. "Pit's a funny name for a dog."

"That's because he's a bottomless pit when it comes to food. He eats all the time."

Lily put her hand to her mouth and giggled. A second later Shannon thought she heard low laughter rumble from Jared's broad chest.

It was the first encouraging sign she had seen since he sat down, but it didn't mean he was willing to give her another chance. She touched Lily's shoulder. "Sweetheart, we need to be going."

"But, Mama, I wanna hear about the dogs. And you said we might stay here."

"I know," Shannon said, handing Lily the lightweight jacket she had left in the booth. Then she looked straight into Jared's eyes. "But we can't stay."

He didn't looked away, but he didn't disagree.

Then she picked up the ticket for their lunches, and carefully counted out the change.

"Hey there, sweet pea." From the other end of the counter Wynette waved to Lily and Shannon realized the waitress was probably trying to tempt the child so the adults could continue their conversation. She couldn't know it was a wasted effort. "How 'bout a candy bar for the road?" she asked, glancing over at Shannon for permission.

When Shannon looked dubious, Wynette added, "It's on the house."

"Thank you. Be sure to thank Mrs. Dickerson, Lily." But the child was already halfway to the counter.

Shannon gathered her purse and Lily's backpack, and slipped out of the booth. Again she looked Jared in the eyes. "I'd give anything to go back and start over, but . . ." She held out her hand. "I'm very sorry for all the trouble I've caused you. I hope you find the woman you're looking for. Goodbye, Jared."

The instant he took her hand, he knew it was a mistake. She had already tapped into his protective instincts, despite the fact that she had lied. But when his wide, rough hand enveloped hers he felt her tremble.

Shannon slipped her hand from his, and walked over to where Wynette waited with Lily.

Conflicting emotions warred inside Jared. Part of him wanted to let her walk out of his life without a backward glance. Part of him wanted her to stay. He couldn't explain it, but he was as attracted to Shannon

Kramer's strength, and even her tardy integrity as he was put off by the fact that she had lied in the first place. He hadn't missed the little gesture of pride when she announced they were leaving, her narrow shoulders shifting ever so slightly beneath the faded denim jacket she wore. Proud enough to cut her losses with dignity, yet humble enough to try any avenue if it meant something better for her child.

A complicated woman.

But if his feelings for Shannon were as complicated as the woman herself, his feelings for her daughter were startlingly simple. Lily was a beautiful, charming child. He had no idea where her father was, but the man was a fool to let such a treasure slip through his fingers.

After paying the bill, and saying goodbye to Wynette, Shannon and Lily walked across the street to the service station and garage that doubled as a bus depot. With every step she prayed that the waitress was right— that once Jared had a chance to think it over, he might not be so upset. And maybe, just maybe, he might change his mind. There was some time left. Their bus didn't leave for another forty-five minutes. And if he didn't change his mind . . .

Well, she thought with a bone-weary sigh, she had been desperate when she arrived, and she would leave the same way. She had managed to escape Hal before, she could do it again. She would do whatever she had to do.

Standing by the register Jared watched them until they went inside the Greyhound station.

"You just gonna stand there, or are you goin' after her?"

He turned to face Wynette. "It didn't work out."

"How would you know? You didn't give it a chance."

"She wasn't honest with—"

"Excuse me?" She propped both hands on her narrow hips. "Since when did you become judge and jury? The woman took a helluva detour just to apologize. And when she damn well couldn't afford it."

"What do you mean?"

"She and that child are down to the bottom of the barrel. She's tryin' to get to California so she can do better for them, but Phoenix is as far as her ticket goes. She'd probably had enough if she hadn't been so all-fired determined to do the right thing by you." She turned, and stomped off toward the kitchen, mumbling, "Hardheaded fool."

Jared glanced across the street just as the door to the bus station closed behind Shannon and Lily Kramer. Suddenly the image of Shannon counting out the exact change for her bill, plus a small tip came to mind. And her telling Lily she had no more quarters. The clothes they wore were clean, but clearly worn.

What if Wynette was right? What if making the effort to apologize had put a dent in their funds? Damn, he felt like a first-class jerk. Maybe he should at least offer to reimburse her for the detour. Recalling the stubborn tilt of her chin, he doubted she would take it, but he would feel better if he offered.

"MAMA, MY colors are gone."

"What?" Shannon immediately began checking the bench where she had left their suitcases while they had gone into the café. "Where did you put them, sweetheart?"

"Right there." Lily pointed to her Cinderella coloring book.

Sure enough, the new box of sixteen crayons that had been on top of the book was gone. "Maybe they fell on the floor." Shannon and Lily both looked, but came up empty-handed. "Are you positive that's where you left them?"

"Uh-huh."

Continuing to search, Shannon noticed, for the first time since returning to the depot, a boy of approximately nine or ten behind the counter. He was sitting on the manager's desk wolfing down a cupcake and a soft drink.

"Excuse me," she said. "Have you seen a box of crayons? They were laying right here when we left, but they seem to have disappeared."

The boy looked at her as if he could have cared less. "Whatsa matter? Can't your little girl keep up with her toys?" He took a giant bite of his cupcake, devouring almost half of it at one time.

At that moment, the manager of the garage came back inside from waiting on a customer.

"Pardon me." Holding Lily's hand Shannon came to stand in front of the counter. "My little girl put a box of crayons on the bench, and they seemed to have disappeared. I was just asking this boy if he had—"

"Tommy Ray, you know anything about this little girl's crayons, son?" the man asked, wiping his greasy hands on an equally greasy rag.

The kid grinned what could only be described as a self-satisfied smirk. "Nope. Reckon somebody just musta picked 'em up when I wasn't looking."

"Sorry, ma'am. I been in the garage most of the time, and didn't see anybody come in."

"But they were right here when we left," Shannon insisted.

The station manager gave her a hard look. "Are you sayin' you think my boy took 'em?"

"No, I'm not accusing your son," she said, straightening her shoulders. "But neither am I willing to forget about something I paid good money for and—"

"Maybe your girl misplaced 'em." Then he leaned across the counter, and gazed down at Lily. "I reckon you better learn to take better care of your things, little miss."

"And I suggest you pick on someone your own size," said a voice from behind Shannon.

She spun about to find Jared Markham not three feet away.

The manager straightened. "Hey, Jared," he said a little nervously. "Whatcha up to?"

"Just checking to make sure Ms. Kramer and her daughter are all right."

"Oh, uh, sure. We was just tryin' to find the little girl's crayons." He threw the rag at the boy. "Go help her look, Tommy Ray."

"But, Daddy—"

"Go help her."

"Never mind. They're replaceable. Are these yours?" Jared asked Shannon, pointing to the suitcases.

"Yes. And just who do you think is going to replace them? Do you have any idea—"

He picked up the suitcases he'd indicated, and started for the door.

"Excuse me? What do you think you're doing?" she demanded.

"Taking you home with me."

"But I thought—"

"Changed my mind."

The minute he had walked in and found Tom Garland glaring down at Lily, the decision had been made for him. Shannon and her daughter needed someone to look out for them, and it looked as if he was the best candidate.

"Well, maybe I have, too," Shannon announced.

Jared stopped, turned to face her. "Have what?"

"Changed my mind. Ten minutes ago I did everything but beg to stay, and all I got from you was a stone face. Why the change of heart?" She couldn't believe she was questioning her good fortune, but she wasn't about to go with him until she knew why he had changed his mind. Call it pride, call it lunacy, but it was important to her.

"You look like you need help."

"I do, but I don't need pity, and I—we—don't go where we're not wanted."

Jared took one look at the stubborn tilt of her chin and knew she wouldn't let him off without showing at least as much courage as she had shown by her personal apology.

He shifted his weight from one foot to the other, and said simply, "You're wanted."

3

JARED MARKHAM had a strange way of showing someone they were wanted. He hadn't said more than twenty
words since tossing the suitcase into the back of his
truck, and helping Shannon and Lily inside, two of
those words being the abbreviated question, "Buckled
up?" right before they pulled away from the bus station. Not only had he been semisilent, but he had
scarcely given her a glance.

Maybe he was already regretting his decision to take
her and Lily along? Maybe he was trying to think of an
appropriate way to dump them? Or maybe, like her, he
just didn't know what to say. In any event, Lily had
taken up the slack by talking about their bus trip to Alpine, but even her charm hadn't moved Jared to much
more than a few nods, some yeahs and maybes, and one
smile. Eventually, mother and daughter both gave up.
Lily played with her doll, and Shannon turned her attention to the scenery. The only sounds came from occasional static on the two-way radio that she assumed
was on constantly due to his job.

Sitting in the cab of the air-conditioned pickup, for
the first time she realized that November in Texas
wasn't just warm, it was downright hot. The West Vir-

ginia climate she was accustomed to was more temperate, even cold in the mountains, and more often than not, damp. The area around Alpine, Texas, was hot and dry, almost desertlike, at least in the daytime. Now, as the sun slipped low toward evening, the heat began to subside.

As they left the city limits sign behind, and drove east out of the little town, miles of nothingness stretched out before them. Except for mountains off to the south and northeast, which would have been labeled hills where she came from, the area was mostly flat, and covered with sparse grass and occasional clumps of cactus. Shannon had never seen a spot that looked more barren and desolate. From her perspective it looked like the ragged end of nowhere.

"Can I—"

"May I."

"Play with the dogs when we get there, Mama?" Lily asked, breaking the silence.

"Well, sweetheart—"

"Mack and Pit will be around," Jared told her.

Lily smiled, her eyes fairly dancing. "Oh boy, oh boy, oh boy." She turned to her mother. "Both of them, Mama. I get to see both of them. Will we be there soon, Mr. Markham?"

"Lily, don't pester Mr. Markham." Although to be honest, the same question had popped into Shannon's mind.

"Another twenty minutes."

After twenty minutes that passed like two hours, Jared turned the truck onto a gravel road. They rode for maybe a mile before she got her first glimpse of his home, a two-story Victorian farmhouse set back in a grove of trees. Probably built in the early 1900s, it embodied the Victorian love of vanity complete with a turret, ornamented gables, bay windows and a wrap-around porch. Shannon's first thought was that the architecture looked oddly out of place in the rugged vastness of the land.

Jared braked the truck to a stop near the back of the house, and from what Shannon could see in the growing dusk, a screened-in porch stretched the entire length of the back of the house. There was a screen door then another door leading to what she thought was probably the kitchen.

"My grandfather built this place for my grandmother in 1910," Jared announced, startling her out of her speculation. "It's old, rambling and in need of some work, but it's paid for."

From the screened-in back porch two dogs barked. "Will they play with me?" Lily wanted to know immediately.

Jared unbuckled the squirming girl, then opened his door and scarcely had time to get out himself before Lily scrambled out, and dashed across the yard.

"Lily, be careful," her mother cautioned.

"Mack! Pit!" Jared commanded, and the dogs quieted instantly. "They sound ferocious but they're really a couple of softies. Besides, the door is latched."

"Oh." Shannon breathed a sigh of relief.

By the time they joined Lily, she and the dogs already had the makings of a fine friendship underway, albeit through a screen. Shannon wasn't sure what breed of dogs to expect, but if the masculinity of their owner and the timbre of their barking were any indication, she anticipated setters or maybe even retrievers. What she got was two... well, the term *mixed breed* didn't even begin to cover their appearance. One had a long, wide body, stubby legs and a tail that curled almost up over his rump. His short, caramel-colored coat was slightly bristly indicating the possibility of terrier lineage, but his large round head and squared muzzle resembled that of a chow. The other dog looked as if it might have started out to be a boxer then changed its mind. With long hair and ears, a chocolate brown coat, and a body that could have belonged to a greyhound, he was the antithesis of the other animal. In fact, they looked like a canine version of Abbott and Costello.

Jared unlatched the screen door, and the dogs shot outside, then immediately returned to display their joy at having their master home. It took several moments before the excitement subsided enough for Jared to introduce Mack and Pit to Lily, and for Shannon to realize they really were indeed a couple of softies. The minute Lily reached out to scratch Mack behind the ears, he rolled over on his back, offering his wide belly for scratching instead. Giggling happily, Lily gladly obliged. Pit stood patiently waiting his turn.

"Okay, guys. Enough." With a hand signal he sent them scampering across the yard. They disappeared into the trees now draped by dusk. "They'll be back when it's time for them to be fed," he promised Lily. Then he unlocked the back door. "Go on in, and I'll get your bags."

Once Shannon was inside the roomy old kitchen with its wonderful ceiling-high glass-front cupboard and cheery blue and white colors, she suffered more pangs of doubt. Jared's first wife had cooked in this kitchen. They probably laughed and talked about how their day had gone. She felt like an intruder coming into another woman's house under false pretenses.

Stop, she cautioned herself. If she kept thinking this way, she wouldn't be any good to Lily or herself. Or Jared. If he was willing to accept her, the least she could do was try to make him happy, if only for a while.

"Can I go find the dogs, Mama?"

"Good heavens, no." Shannon brushed a wisp of too-long bangs from Lily's eyes. "It's already dark outside. Tomorrow," she promised, "you'll have lots of time to get acquainted with Mack and Pit."

"But I wanna—" Lily yawned "—be their friend."

Jared came back in just as the child yawned again. "You need to put her to bed?"

"Well, it has been a long day, and—"

"Down that hall, and upstairs," he nodded, holding their suitcase. "First bedroom on your left. I'll be right behind you."

The bedroom was a lovely surprise, with an antique rosewood canopy bed, cheval mirror, dressing table and armoire. The quilt was a star pattern in shades of blues and lavenders, and the pillow shams were crocheted. Shannon was no connoisseur of antiques, but she had been to too many quilting bees as a child not to recognize genuine craftsmanship when she saw it. Someone, possibly Jared's grandmother, had hand stitched everything with great care.

"Mama, look." Lily pointed to the crocheted canopy, then turned to Jared. "Did a princess used to sleep here?"

He tilted his head to one side as if giving the question serious consideration. "Nope. Not that I know of. You're not a princess, are you?"

Lily grinned. "No, I'm a girl."

"Well, then you're in luck because this bed is a girl's bed." He turned to Shannon. "I, uh, wasn't expecting two, so I hope you don't mind doubling—"

"It's fine," she said quickly. "It's...lovely. Thank you."

He set their things down beside the armoire. "After you've tucked Lily in, maybe we could talk in the kitchen."

"Of course."

"Sweet dreams, princess," he told Lily, and was rewarded with a giggly good-night as he left the room.

Jared rammed his hands into his pockets, and headed for the kitchen, the question, *now what?* flashing across his brain like a neon sign. The decision that Shannon and Lily needed rescuing had been born out of pure gut instinct, but now logic was demanding a long hard look at the consequences. How would this situation ever work? How could he trust her after she had lied to him?

Her lie. Mentally, he kept tripping over it like the upturned corner of a rug. It was irritating to say the least. Why couldn't she have just been honest? Okay, so a few men had given her a bad time. That didn't give her license to omit something as important as having a child. Logically, he never should have . . .

What? Brought her home? If he used that basis for logic he probably never should have written the ad in the first place. But nothing about this situation was logical. His instant decision to bring them to his home had proved that. So, she hadn't told him everything for fear of being rejected. Now that he'd had time to think about it, he could understand. But logic and understanding aside, in the final analysis he was a man that relied on his instincts. In his job, intuition often played as big a role as good solid police work. Call it following a hunch, or just a feeling in the gut, it all amounted to the same thing: the small voice inside that whispered you were on the right track. Or off.

Jared's instincts had rarely been wrong, and right now they were telling him to give Shannon Kramer a chance.

When Shannon joined Jared almost a half hour later, the kitchen was filled with the aroma of fresh-brewed coffee. He was at the table, a full mug in his hand, another waiting for her.

"Is she asleep?" he asked.

"Practically before her head touched the pillow. It's been a long day for her." And a nerve-racking one for me, Shannon thought.

He nodded. "I, uh, wasn't sure how you took your coffee."

"A little cream." He pointed toward a creamer already sitting on the table. "Thanks." She doctored her coffee, and waited for him to speak. Again, she wondered if he had changed his mind, and was trying to find some way to let her down gently.

Jared cleared his throat. "Would you, uh, like to take our coffee and go outside to the porch?"

"Sure." She followed him out the back door.

He flipped a light switch beside the door, but nothing happened. "Oh, hell," he muttered. "I'll get a bulb, and be right back."

"We don't need it."

He jerked his head around. "What?"

"There's a full moon, and it's bright as day out here."

"Oh, yeah, it is." Lord, he thought, would they ever get past this awkwardness?

Good grief, she thought, what if she gave him the idea she didn't *want* the light on? What if he thought she was sending him some kind of sexual message? "Of course, if you'd rather have the light on, it's okay."

"No, the moonlight is more than enough." He walked to a small table with two chairs, and pulled one out for her.

"Thanks," she said, clasping the cup in both hands to hide her nervousness.

After a few seconds of silence, he said, "I'm not sure what the proper etiquette is for our situation, so I'm just going to think out loud." She nodded, and he continued. "I thought maybe a trial period would be a good idea. Say four weeks, or six if you need longer."

"Six . . ." Shannon said a silent prayer of thanks. He hadn't changed his mind! "Six weeks sounds fine to—to me." It sounded better than fine, it sounded wonderful. If she and Lily could stay hidden for six weeks, surely they could shake Hal off their trail for good.

"That should give us time to get to know each other."

"Yes, I think so."

"And then we'll . . . sort of see how it goes, if that's all right with you?"

"It's fine."

"Good." He took a deep breath, clearly relieved to have at least that much out of the way. "You, uh, mentioned that Lily is five, so I suppose that means kindergarten. I don't know how you want to handle school, but there's a bus—"

"I home school Lily."

"Oh?"

The note of surprise in his voice almost sounded as if he doubted her capability. Hal had always assumed she didn't have two brain cells to rub together. It was one of the things she disliked most about him. Her defenses went up like the hackles on a hound's back.

"You don't have to be a certified teacher to home school," she snapped.

"I didn't mean..." She had obviously taken his comment the wrong way. "Look," he said. "This situation comes with ready-made stress, and I sure don't want to add to that. If I offended you just now—"

Shannon held up her hand. "No. It wasn't you, it was me. Sometimes I react defensively when it's not necessary. I apologize." She gave him a small smile. "Habit, I guess. And you're right. We've got enough to deal with without looking for trouble. I think the best thing we can do is keep an open mind and a positive attitude."

"Absolutely. There's only one thing I ask of you. It's very important that we be as honest with each other as possible. Otherwise, for me at least, this won't work."

"How many ways can I apologize? I *am* sorry that I didn't tell you about Lily from the beginning."

"And I've accepted your apology. So, we start fresh from here. No more lies. Agreed?"

"Agreed."

Having reached their agreement they both fell silent. Night sounds crowded in around them. Crickets chirped, and she worried the handle of her cup with the pad of her thumb. In the distance a coyote barked, and Jared drummed the fingers of his right hand against the side of his mug.

Finally, Shannon said, "I was wondering . . ."

He raised the mug to his lips, finishing the coffee in one long swallow. Watching the muscles in his neck, she was again struck by the sheer power of this man who was both stranger and savior.

"Wondering what?"

"What?" she said, realizing she was staring at his neck. "Oh. I was uh, wondering if you would mind if I asked you some questions?"

"What kind of questions?"

"About your job?"

"Ask away."

"Well, I think I have a good idea of what a game warden does, but I'm not sure."

"You think we issue hunting licenses and camping permits, right?"

"Something like that."

"That's part of it, but the bulk of my time is spent dealing with poachers."

"You mean like hunting out of season?"

"And trapping. Everything from deer, fox and big-horn sheep to cactus."

"Cactus?"

He grinned at her shocked expression. "Believe it or not, it's a big business. The yucca and barrel varieties

particularly. Some of the large ones can bring anywhere from two to three hundred dollars in landscape
areas like California and Florida. And since it's illegal
to transport any species of cacti out of the state, that's
where I come in. A game warden is a law enforcement
officer the same as a sheriff, state trooper, or any policeman. When someone breaks the law, it's my job to
apprehend them."

"Do you arrest people . . . the poachers?"

"Certainly. If we can find them."

"What do you mean?"

"Brewster County has over six thousand square
miles, and only two game wardens. It's not unusual for
a report of poachers to come in, and by the time I get
there, they've disappeared."

"That's a lot of territory to cover for only two men."

"It'd be almost impossible without the complete co-
operation of the ranchers around here. They're usually
the ones calling in the violation, and more often than
not they keep an eye on the perpetrators until a warden
arrives. Other times, we happen upon violators while
on patrol."

"You mean while the poachers are in the act?"

"Yes."

"That sounds so dangerous."

"It can be."

"Do these people ever have guns?"

"Frequently."

The thought of Jared facing off with some Uzi-toting smuggler suddenly made Shannon's blood run cold. She didn't like thinking of him in danger.

"How, uh, long have you been a game warden?" she asked, wanting to shake the disturbing images in her mind. Images of Jared hurt or worse.

"Over ten years."

"Well, you obviously love your work."

"Obviously?"

"If not, you would be looking for a new profession instead of a new relationship."

He smiled. "Good point. But it has its drawbacks. In fact, my job is the main reason I contacted the magazine in the first place."

"Because of the remoteness of the locale, and the nature of your job."

"Does that bother you?"

"I'm not a bright lights, big city kind of person, and I love the outdoors."

"Well, we've certainly got plenty of the great outdoors."

Shannon smiled. "So I noticed."

"I don't mean to get too personal, but I need to ask how you feel about spending a lot of time on your own. If I get a call, it could mean I'll be out all night."

Shannon glanced down at the coffee now cold in her cup. "I'm used to taking care of myself, Jared."

"No offense, but there's a lot of difference between taking care of yourself in the city, and out here."

She met his gaze directly. "I'm not a whiner, and I don't have a tendency to panic. I'm a good housekeeper, a decent cook, a lousy laundress, and I can probably fire—with a moderate level of skill—any weapon you own."

"Well, I'm a slob, I'll eat just about anything that isn't charred, I send my uniforms to the cleaners, and I'll keep that in mind in case I ever make you mad."

He delivered the quip with such a straight face that for a moment Shannon didn't realize that it was his attempt to ease the tension. Well, what do you know? she thought. Underneath that strong silent facade is a sense of humor. "I think we just had our first meeting of minds."

"How did we do?"

"On a scale of one to ten, I'd say a six plus."

"I'll take it. Shannon," he said a second or two later.

"Yes."

"I'm . . . I'm glad I changed my mind."

"So am I," she said softly.

Again they let the night sounds fill a silence that stretched into long minutes.

Sitting in the moonlight with this man she scarcely knew, yet to whom she had committed herself to spending the next few weeks of her life with, Shannon again wondered what it would be like if all this was real. What would it be like to sit in the moonlight with a man who loved her? A man she could depend on without giving up her independence. The idea was delicious, heady... and pure fantasy. She stole a glance at Jared.

But a lovely fantasy, she thought.

"Well," he said finally. "I guess we'd better turn in. By the way, are you an early riser?"

"With a five-year-old you have no option to be anything else," she said as they walked back inside the house.

He nodded. "I have to patrol the area to the south tomorrow, so I'll be leaving around seven, and won't be back until early afternoon."

"Lily and I will be fine."

He took the empty cup from her, and set it on the kitchen counter along with his. "In the morning I'll show you how to operate the radio in case you need to reach me. As smart as you are, you'll pick it up in no time."

Shannon smiled. "Thanks."

"You're welcome," he said, totally unaware of the compliment he had just paid her.

"Well... good night, Jared."

"Good night, Shannon."

He watched her walk down the hall toward the stairs, her hips swaying ever so slightly. She had the kind of figure most women would label too rounded, while most men would consider it a feast for the eyes. She didn't flaunt it, but then she possessed the kind of earthy sensuality that didn't need flaunting. It made its own statement, like the subtle fragrance of a single gardenia in a garden of roses.

That sensuality had been startlingly evident as they sat on the porch. He remembered how the moonlight seemed to caress her face, and thinking that her full mouth looked soft, warm, and made for kissing.

Jared tried to shake himself free of such thoughts, concentrating on making sure the dogs were secure for the night. Success was limited, due to the fact that he kept thinking about Shannon's mouth. How could he think about kissing her when he had only known her a few hours? He hadn't kissed Amy until their second date. But then he was relatively certain, even on such short acquaintance, that Shannon was nothing like Amy. Physically, there were some similarities—a pretty face, long dark hair—otherwise, they were as opposite as daylight and darkness. Amy had a fragile, almost ethereal quality about her that always evoked his protective instincts. On the other hand, while Shannon was definitely soft and womanly, Jared sensed she had a strength that Amy never possessed. The kind of strength required to even contemplate a relationship with a stranger if it meant a better life for her child. A substantive quality his great-grandmother would have called good old-fashioned grit.

Yet despite her strength, she was vulnerable. He'd seen it in her eyes when she reacted so defensively about home schooling Lily. Oh, there had been anger, too. But mixed in with the anger flashing in her eyes, he thought he caught a glimpse of fear. Fear of what? he wondered. What, or who, had taught her to feel she needed to be on guard? One moment he was a little shocked to realize how little he knew about this woman he had invited into his life. The next moment he admitted there was something . . . exciting about not knowing, about the prospect of discovering just exactly who Shannon was, what she liked or didn't like. How she felt about politics, religion and the price of tea in China. She intrigued him.

Again, he couldn't help but compare her to Amy. He and Amy had known each other all their lives. They were friends long before they became lovers, and that friendship was one of the strongest parts of their marriage.

Stop measuring one by the other, he told himself. They were two different women in two totally different circumstances. What bothered him was not so much the differences between the two women, but the fact that the memory of Amy's delicate beauty paled next to Shannon's understated, but nonetheless potent sensuality. A sensuality he was finding it difficult to ignore after almost two years of celibacy.

4

"OH!" SHANNON whipped around at the sound of footsteps, her heart hammering in her chest. Automatically, she stepped back, and bumped into the edge of the kitchen counter.

"I didn't mean to scare you," Jared said.

"I . . . you . . ." She swallowed hard, clutching the lapels of her thin cotton robe together. "I came down to—"

"Take a deep breath," he advised.

Shannon did, and felt a little calmer. "I heard your shower running, and I thought I would make you some coffee before you went to work. But I couldn't find the coffee, and then you came in—"

"And scared the hell out of you."

She managed a smile. "Something like that."

"Sorry."

"It's . . . it's all right, or at least it will be as soon as my heart rate slows to a mere gallop."

He smiled back, and she thought again how truly good-looking he was, more so when he smiled.

"Guess I could wear a bell. You know, like a house cat."

Standing there with the early morning sunlight glinting off his badge pinned to one of the broadest chests she had ever seen, the last image he evoked was of a domesticated feline. A tiger maybe, all power and prowl, but definitely not a house cat.

She clutched the robe tighter, suddenly aware that the hemline fell at midthigh, exposing a good deal of her bare legs and feet. For a moment she thought about dashing back upstairs to dress, then decided it would only make the situation more awkward. She might as well just tough it out. "If you'll, uh, show me where you keep everything, I'll brew a pot of coffee."

"Deal. Mine tastes like sludge. One sip, and you'd be headed for the bus stop as fast as you could get there."

"It wasn't that bad last night."

"I guess I was lucky. But usually, it's pretty brutal. Ask Wynette," he suggested, walking straight to where she stood. "She swears it's lethal." He reached over her head, flipped open a cabinet, and retrieved a two-pound can of coffee. "Guess I'll have to do some rearranging. Make sure the things you need are within your reach."

"Or loan me a stepladder." He handed her the coffee. "Thanks."

"You're welcome." He glanced down at her bare feet. "This old linoleum floor can be downright cold in the morning. You might want to remember your slippers."

He was so close.

Her throat went dry, and Shannon had to will her suddenly racing heart to quiet. She hadn't been alone with a man since her divorce, and her first instinct was to flee. Logically, she knew not all men were like her ex-husband, but emotionally she wanted to run like hell. But this man wasn't Hal. And she had made a promise to herself never again to allow anyone, male or female, to treat her as he had. Not that she had turned against men. There had been invitations, which she refused unless they included Lily. But standing here, close enough to smell Jared's after-shave made her realize how much she longed for the kind of intimacy that had only been a dream until now. Someday, when she was sure Hal was out of the picture, she would have it. And with a man like Jared.

"Shannon?"

"What? Oh, yes...slippers. I'll remember," she said, clutching the can of coffee to her chest.

"The pot is in that cupboard."

"Thanks." In less than five minutes the first drops of dark, rich brew began filling the glass carafe. "I'll, uh, be back in a jiffy," Shannon said, and rushed upstairs to dress.

Lily was still asleep so she collected her clothes, and went into the bathroom. Dressing quickly in jeans, a T-shirt and sneakers, she headed back downstairs to fix breakfast. As she walked into the kitchen the sound of a familiar small voice announced the fact that her daughter was not only awake, but jabbering like a magpie, with an audience to boot. Standing over a pan of sizzling bacon, Jared looked as if he were hanging on every word. Even Mack and Pit were listening, their heads cocked attentively.

"Mama, Mama." A tea towel tied over her pajamas as a makeshift apron, a piece of bacon in her hand, Lily danced across the floor to give her mother a hug. "I'm helping Jared fix breakfast. Didya know sometimes Pit and Mack go in the truck, and they smell bad people sometimes so they can..." She glanced over her shoulder at Jared.

"Track," he supplied.

"Yeah. So they can track. They do it with their noses." The child pointed to her own nose. "Jared said so," she proclaimed, clearly proud of herself.

"I hope you don't mind me giving her permission to drop the Mr. Markham. Manners are important, but under the circumstances—"

"No, that's perfectly okay. You're right. Under the circumstances, it was a bit formal."

"Good."

Shannon brushed back a lock of hair that fell over her eyes. She had dressed in such a hurry that she hadn't taken the time to do her usual French braid. "I thought you might expect me to cook."

"Can you?"

"Well, Julia Child doesn't have anything to fear, but I'm a fair hand at a stove."

"Mama cooks cookies the best."

"Bakes cookies," Shannon corrected.

"With chocolate chips?" Jared asked.

"Lots and lots," Lily assured him.

"That's all the reference I need. Be my guest." He handed her the tongs he had been using to turn the bacon. "I'm really tired of my own cooking anyway. Eggs are in that bowl ready to scramble, and the toaster is already loaded with English muffins. All you have to do is push down the lever."

"Do you eat like this every day?" She threw a dollop of butter into the second skillet, and poured in the beaten eggs. Then she started the muffins toasting.

"Nope. Too much fat." He patted his ridiculously flat midsection. "But my pint-size guest made a special request. Of course, I couldn't refuse such a charming young lady."

Shannon looked at Lily. "Little con artist." But Lily only grinned.

"I, uh, hope you don't mind, but I asked Wynette to drop by later this morning to kind of show you the ropes. You know, where everything is, how everything runs." Eager for her not to take offense as she had last night, he quickly added, "Not that you couldn't figure it all out for yourself, but I thought it might save you some time. She cleans for me every week and—"

"If you'd like, I can do that while I'm here." She divided the scrambled eggs between three plates, adding the bacon just about the time the muffins popped up.

"I appreciate the offer, but Wynette and Ellis—that's her husband—fell on hard times last year when he broke his hip. Their daughter and son-in-law moved in to help work the ranch, and Wynette went to work at the café to bring in extra money. Since she and Ellis would starve before they would take anything that even remotely resembled charity, having her clean house doesn't dent her pride, and it lets me help in a small way."

Shannon handed Lily her breakfast, instructing her to carry it carefully to the table. "I'm sorry. I didn't know."

"How could you?"

"Jared."

"Yes." He took the filled plate she handed him.

"You don't have to qualify everything you say to me. I realize you're probably a little gun-shy after I practically bit your head off last night, but I don't want you to think you need to tiptoe around me. My feelings aren't all that fragile, really."

"All right, no tiptoeing." But he wasn't so sure about the fragile part. No one learned to be so protective without having a few scars to show for their knowledge. He was beginning to wonder if her strength shielded a wounded heart. Another intriguing facet of Shannon Kramer? And how many more were there?

IMMEDIATELY AFTER breakfast Lily had dashed upstairs to dress, then downstairs to play with Mack and Pit on the back porch. Satisfied her child was safe and entertained, Shannon followed Jared into his office so that he could show her how to operate the radio.

"Sit here." He patted the back of an aging leather chair in front of his desk. "Now," he said once she was seated, "this is a transmitter and a receiver. That simply means you can talk to me, and I can talk back. I carry a handheld mobile unit with me whenever I leave the truck."

"All you have to do . . ." He leaned forward, and for a wild heartbeat or two she fought the familiar urge to bolt from the chair, to get as far away from him as she could. But the feeling passed surprisingly quick.

"I think . . . I think I've got that."

"Good. Now, there are three repeaters in the county so this unit has no trouble reaching me anywhere, unless I'm in a hole."

"A hole? That doesn't sound good."

"It's not as bad as it sounds. Once in a while when I'm tracking I wind up between two large rock formations or down in a low spot, hence the name. When that happens, the signal cuts out. It's rare, and nothing for you to worry about."

"If you say so."

"I do."

"But how will I be able to hear you on this radio if I'm in the kitchen or out in the backyard?"

"There's an extra mobile unit. Same frequencies. Okay, let's go over it again, only this time you show me."

While she did her best to repeat what he had just taught her, he squatted beside her, balancing himself on the balls of his feet. "Very good," he said when she had finished. "See, I knew you could pick this up in a flash."

"Thanks. I had—" she turned, and found his face barely a foot away from hers, "—an excellent teacher."

His size and proximity should have made her nervous. And it did, but not for the reason she expected. Instead of feeling threatened, she basked in the warmth of his compliment. There was something oddly comforting about having this brawny man praise her.

Gracious, but his eyes are blue, she thought. Like a cloudless late summer sky. And his mouth was, well . . . *beautiful* was the first word that popped into her head. Sculpted like one of those Greek statues. The same could be said of his jaw and chin. Strength in every line, right down to the cleft in his chin.

"You think you've got it now?" Did she know how sweet she looked, he wondered. Her face was free of cosmetics, her hair just the least bit tousled. The package was charming, and more appealing than he was prepared for.

"Yes."

"Don't ever hesitate to call if you need me."

"Okay."

"Even if all you want to do is chat for a while. I'm concerned you may get bored, just you and Lily by yourselves."

"We're used to being by ourselves, but thanks for your concern."

"You're also used to depending on no one but yourself, aren't you?"

"I suppose so."

Their heads were so close he could almost feel her breath on his cheek. Despite the fact that they were still virtually strangers, as he gazed into her green eyes he had a powerful urge to say, Depend on me.

"Shannon." He said her namely so softly it was almost a whisper. "I . . . I want to tell you—"

"Mama, Mama, we got company," Lily called from the doorway.

The two adults looked up to find Wynette standing beside the child. Normally, Shannon would have corrected her daughter's grammar, but at the moment all rules on tense and diction seemed to have evaporated from her brain. She wasn't sure she liked the idea that Jared could distract her so easily.

"Well, don't you two look cozy," Wynette said, grinning.

Jared stood up. "I was just showing Shannon how to operate the radio."

"Looked like you were doin' a little operatin' yourself," she teased.

Jared wasn't certain but out of the corner of his eye he thought he saw a blush stain Shannon's cheek. As for himself, he decided it was a good thing he wasn't wearing a tie because he would definitely need to loosen it.

"By the way," Wynette said. "Ellis and I figured Shannon would need some wheels while she's here, so Ellis said you could borrow that old Chevy truck of his if you want." She turned to Shannon. "Ain't much to look at. No air-conditioning but it'll get you to Alpine and back for whatever errands you need to run."

"That's very kind of you. I appreciate it."

"Uh, yeah. Tell Ellis I said, thanks. Well, uh, guess I better get moving. You ladies get acquainted, and I'll see you this afternoon."

"Bye-bye." Lily smiled up at him.

He swooped her up into his arms. "So long, princess. You keep Mack and Pit out of trouble, okay."

She nodded enthusiastically.

He set Lily on her feet, paused for a second to glance back at Shannon, then left. Watching his broad shoulders disappear she had an overwhelmingly wifely urge to tell him to be careful.

"Well, that's a load off my mind," Wynette said.

"What?" Shannon had almost forgotten the other woman was there.

"I was gettin' downright worried. Plum scared in fact, that I wasn't ever gonna see that look in his eyes again."

"What look?"

"The me-Tarzan-you-Jane look."

Shannon blushed. "Now, sugar, don't go bashful on me. I'm tickled pink. It's about time he put the past behind him, and started living for himself again."

"Y-you mean because his wife died." Shannon had never been one to pry into anyone else's personal life, but she had to admit that she was curious about Jared's late wife. What had she been like? What had they been like together?

"Took it real hard, that man did. For a while me and Ellis thought he was gonna curl up and die himself. Never seen a man go so silent. I swear, it was almost like if he didn't talk about it, he could pretend it wasn't true. But then, a double blow like that is almost more than a body can stand."

"A double blow?"

"Uh..." Wynette frowned, and quickly glanced away. "Listen to me jabberin' on. Why don't we go to the kitchen, and I can give you the fifty-cent tour. And you, sweet pea," she said, tweaking Lily's nose, "have got a treat comin'. I've got a brand-new colorin' book and crayons in my bag just for you."

"Yippee." Lily jumped up and down. "New colors."

"Well, then let's go get 'em."

As she followed Wynette out, Shannon wondered what she could have meant by a double blow.

BY NOON SHANNON felt as if she had known Wynette
for years. The older woman had an easy way about her,
and soon they were talking like old friends. It wasn't
difficult to see that she had more or less adopted Jared
since his wife's death. And although Wynette didn't ignore his faults, there was no doubt that she considered
him to be the son she'd never had. To quote her, "He
was the best catch in Brewster County, bar none." As
far as Shannon could tell, her new friend was right on
the money.

"I'm surprised the women around here haven't been
beating down Jared's door," Shannon told Wynette as
they were preparing lemonade and tuna sandwiches for
their lunch.

"Well, first off, you'd be surprised at how few single
women there are around here. But don't think the ones
that are didn't pester him."

"Yet he decided to advertise for a woman."

"Wife," Wynette said, snagging slices of bread as they
popped out of the toaster. "What Jared needs is someone who'll stick with him, who'll stand beside him on
her own two feet. And to answer your question, he
doesn't have time to go courtin'. The man gets one day
a week off, and it's nearly forty miles to the nearest
town. Besides, everybody around here knows everybody else, and he didn't want a woman who had known
Amy." She shrugged. "Just didn't feel right about that,
I guess."

"Amy?" Shannon put the freshly made pitcher of lemonade in the refrigerator. "Was that his wife's name?"

"Yep. Pretty as a peach blossom, and dainty as a china teacup. She had a big heart, though. Lord, but she loved Jared. They were sweethearts from the time they were in grammar school, and there was never anyone else for either of 'em. Quite a match. The preacher's daughter, and the son of one of the county's oldest families."

Shannon knew she shouldn't be so curious about Jared's life with his late wife, but she couldn't stop herself. "Jared told me his grandfather built this house."

"Oh, sugar, there've been Markhams in this part of Texas since the Civil War. Most of 'em were policemen or politicians. Did Jared tell you his grandfather served two terms in the state legislature?"

"No. Does he have a lot of family?"

"Just a brother, who lives in Wyoming. His mom passed on about ten years ago, and his dad a couple of years later." Wynette shook her head. "That boy's seen a fair amount of grief," she said almost to herself.

"I suppose you knew his wife well?"

"Oh, yeah. She—"

Mack's and Pit's sharp barking cut her off. "That would be Donna Jean," Wynette said, wiping her hands on a tea towel as she headed for the back door.

A moment later she returned with a young woman in tow, carrying a cake. Lily was close behind. "Shannon Kramer, this is my daughter, Donna Jean. And this," Wynette gently patted her daughter's extremely rounded belly, "is my future grandchild."

"Pleased to meetcha." Donna Jean, a lovely blonde in her early twenties smiled warmly.

"Nice to meet you. Both of you."

Donna Jean laughed. "I hope you like chocolate." She held up the cake. "I know it's Jared's favorite."

"I like chocolate a whole bunch," Lily piped up.

"Thanks," Shannon took the cake and set it on the counter. "And as you can see, it certainly won't go to waste. Donna Jean, this is my daughter, Lily."

"Hi there," Donna Jean said, but Lily's attention was focused on the three-layer confection frosted in dark chocolate fudge icing. "If your mama says it's okay, would you like the first piece?"

Lily's eyes lit up like firecrackers in the night sky as she turned to her mother. "Only after your lunch," Shannon said.

"Yippee! Chocolate cake."

"You've made her day," Shannon told the young woman. "It was a very neighborly gesture, but from the look of things you should probably be resting, not baking."

"Naw, I get bored doin' nothing. Too much like my mama, I guess."

In response Wynette playfully snapped the tea towel at Donna Jean's backside. "We're just about to eat. You wanna join us for a sandwich?"

"Please." Shannon pulled a chair out from the kitchen table. "And I really would feel better if you sat down."

"Mama, can I take my samich to the porch?" Lily asked.

"Wouldn't recommend it with Pit out there waitin' for the first crumb to drop. Matter of fact," Wynette warned, "you look away once, and he'll take the whole darn thing."

As if to confirm the warning, Pit licked his chops on the other side of the screen.

"Now, don't give me that look," Shannon said at Lily's droopy expression. "After lunch you can go right back out to play. Deal?"

"Deal." Lily agreed, but her acquiescence was hardly overflowing with enthusiasm.

Wynette got the sandwiches and some potato chips while Shannon brought the lemonade from the refrigerator. They were just about to enjoy their meal when Jared came home.

"Well, looks like I didn't arrive a minute too soon," he said from the kitchen doorway. They had been so busy talking none of them had heard him come in. "Got an extra sandwich?

"Of course. There's plenty of tuna. It'll just take a second to make more sandwiches."

"I'll do it, Mama," Donna Jean offered. "I'm not real hungry anyway." With considerable difficulty she began maneuvering herself out of the chair.

"No!"

Shannon and Lily looked up, shocked at the tone in Jared's voice.

"No. Don't you dare get up." For a moment Shannon thought she saw fear in his eyes.

"But it's no trouble—"

"I mean it, Donna Jean. Don't you even think about getting up out of that chair to wait on me or anyone else."

"Oh, Jared. You're worse than Mama."

"Well, this time he's right," Wynette lifted an eyebrow, and wagged a finger at Jared. "And don't let *that* go to your head."

Shannon smiled at the teasing jibe but she couldn't help noticing that Jared's body was as tense as his voice had been. For half a heartbeat he'd seemed ready to rush across the floor and make Donna Jean stay put. Then he relaxed, as if Wynette's snappy retort had broken the tension.

It crossed her mind that perhaps he and Donna Jean had been an item before he married, but then she remembered that Wynette had told her Jared and Amy were sweethearts from grade school. They had never dated anyone else. Then why, she wondered, was he so obviously concerned? Had Donna Jean had a difficult pregnancy? Wynette didn't appear to be overly worried. What was Jared's problem?

"C'mon, Jared. Relax." Donna Jean put a hand on her expanded waist. "And that's an order."

While Lily gobbled her sandwich, Shannon watched Jared, and tried to figure out what was going on.

"Have you given any more thought to my offer?" he asked.

"No. I'm fine. The baby's fine," the new mother-to-be said firmly. "And there's no reason to worry."

"But what if—"

Donna Jean held up her hand. "Jared, Neal and I appreciate everything you've done, but please don't go crazy over this."

Wynette pushed her chair away from the table. "Short trip if you ask me. You finished, sweet pea?" When Lily nodded, her mouth still full, Wynette shooed her outside. That appeared to be the signal to drop the topic because Donna Jean immediately began telling Shannon all about her latest purchase for the nursery while Wynette made Jared a sandwich.

Shannon still wasn't sure what was going on, but she had the strangest feeling that it had to do with some kind of past disaster. Maybe Donna Jean had lost a baby before, and that's where the concern came from. But if that was the case, why did Jared seem to be more concerned than the young woman's own mother?

The rest of the meal passed uneventfully until Donna Jean rose, a bit unsteadily, to leave. In a flash Jared was at her side, assisting her. "You know, I can't even remember what my toes look like or what it's like to get out of a chair under my own steam," she said rubbing the small of her back.

Shannon smiled. "Believe me, none of this discomfort will matter the minute they put that little baby in your arms."

Donna Jean grinned. "Yeah. I can't wait. Three more weeks the doctor says." She waddled over to give her mother a peck on the cheek then said goodbye to Shannon. Jared offered to walk her to her truck, but she declined, and left. For several moments he stood at the back door, watching until Donna Jean drove away.

Shannon felt like such an outsider. As if she had eavesdropped on a conversation she wasn't supposed to hear. Yet, at the same time, she wasn't angry at the exclusion because it hadn't been deliberate. Jared's reaction had been so quick, so spontaneous that it couldn't have been.

"Here you go." Wynette set the plate with Jared's sandwich on the table.

He turned around. "What? Oh, thanks." He glanced at his watch. "Better take it with me. I forgot I promised Dale Thompson I would check out the two mule deer he found shot on his property."

Then he met Shannon's gaze for the first time since he'd walked into the kitchen. "I'm sorry about...about lunch."

She wasn't sure if he was apologizing for what had happened or for excluding her, or both. "It's okay."

He started to speak, then hesitated, and before he could change his mind, Wynette walked up and handed him the sandwich sealed in a plastic bag.

"I, uh, probably won't be home until almost six. If you and Lily get hungry, don't wait on me."

"Lily's appetite is hard to stall, but I'll wait. We can have dinner together."

"I'll look forward to it."

HE WAS EARLY, and carrying flowers. "These are just wildflowers, but I thought you might like to put them on the table."

"They're lovely, Jared. Thank you." She sniffed the bouquet of sunny fragrances all mingled together.

"Where's the princess?"

"Upstairs with the new coloring book you so graciously asked Wynette to bring when she came today. That was a very sweet thing to do."

"My pleasure. I'll just say hello, wash up, and be right back. By the way," he said over his shoulder, "whatever you're cooking smells delicious."

"Hope you can still say that after you've tasted it."

A few minutes later she could hear him upstairs with Lily. They were laughing. Shannon couldn't help but smile. She found it hard to believe that two days ago she had never laid eyes on Jared. Now here she was cooking for him, her child was laughing with him, and it all seemed completely normal. As if they had done this every evening for years.

If Jared had expected a quiet dinner for two, Shannon thought, he was disappointed. Not that he looked disappointed as Lily regaled him with practically everything she had seen and done throughout the day. And of course, the dogs played a big part in her monologue. He sat patiently listening while eating his meal, and even managed appropriate responses.

"Wow," he said, when she told him how high she could jump, and "I'll bet that was fun." And his wide-eyed comment, "You got Mack and Pit to fetch a stick. That's amazing!" totally impressed Lily.

Seeing her daughter so enthralled was a bittersweet pain in Shannon's heart. Bitter because it cast a harsh light on how starved Lily was for attention from a gentle man, and the fact that she had certainly never received it from her own father. And sweet because Jared didn't even have to work at being attentive. He simply cared.

He would make a wonderful father. Call it woman's intuition or a mother's instinct, but she knew Jared would be a loving committed parent. And after watching him with Lily, it wasn't much of a leap to imagine the scene was for real. To imagine that she and Lily could have this kind of life—safe and secure, with a husband and father that cared—was the dream she held dear, but one she feared would never be a reality.

And now she saw that dream in her daughter's eyes.

A dream. A hope.

To her shame and horror, Shannon suddenly realized she had done her child an unforgivable injustice. Lily was so wrapped up in Jared. How would she feel after living with him—with his kindness and affection—for six weeks? Shannon caught her breath at the adoring look in her daughter's eyes. Lily had bonded with Jared. And the bond was stronger than Shannon could have ever imagined.

What had she done?

How could she not have realized the effect this unorthodox situation would have on Lily?

She had jumped at Jared's ad like a falling mountain climber grabbing for a lifeline. Without any thought to possible damage to her daughter's emotional stability. What kind of mother was she? How could she have ignored the obvious consequences?

The answer, of course, was fear. She had been operating out of fear for so long that it had become the motivation for everything she thought, everything she did. The fear never left her. It was like living with an invisible third person, always present, always out of sight, but never out of mind.

She couldn't let Lily continue to build her hopes around Jared, and then yank her away. They had to leave, and the sooner the better.

"Shannon?"

"What?" She had been so deep into thought that she hadn't realized Lily had left the table.

"Are you all right?"

"Of course," she assured him, forcing a smile. Meanwhile her mind was whirling. How was she going to tell him that they were leaving? She rose from the table, picked up both of their plates, and took them to the sink. As she passed the door, she stuck her head through, and called to Lily, telling her it was almost bath time.

"You're upset about what happened at lunch, aren't you?"

"Oh . . ." She set the plates down so fast they clattered on the tiled counter top. "No, that's not—"

"I don't blame you. What I did was rude, and unforgivable. Please accept my apology."

"It's not necessary."

"Yes, it is. You see, I'm a little overprotective about Donna Jean and her pregnancy. We grew up together, and she's a good friend. I'd do just about anything to make sure she was okay."

"That's what being a good friend is all about."

He nodded. "But I can't let it go at that. I'm afraid for her."

"I think it's only natural. Babies are born every day, but not to your friend."

"No. You don't understand. I'm afraid something will happen to her and her baby."

For the first time she looked closely at him. He was so tense the muscles in his neck stood out, and there was a line of perspiration along his upper lip. She had been so wrapped up in her own thoughts that she hadn't seen how truly distraught he looked until now.

"Jared?" She put her hand on his arm. He was trembling. "I'm sure Donna Jean's doctor is taking good care—"

"Doesn't matter. It can still happen."

"What can happen?"

"She could die."

"Why would you think—"

"Because Amy died."

Shannon gasped. Oh, no, she thought. His wife had died when she was pregnant.

"Sh-she went into labor, and didn't tell me. Something was wrong. I was out on patrol, and she . . ." He swallowed hard. "She waited too long, and it was so far to the hospital. I drove . . . drove as fast as I could but . . ."

Shannon felt the shudder pass through his body, and into hers, and knew what was coming. She wanted to put her hand on his lips to keep the words from spilling out, but knew she couldn't.

"It was too late," he whispered. "For both of them."

5

EVEN KNOWING what he was going to say before he said it didn't make it any easier to hear. No wonder he had been so protective of Donna Jean. He looked at her and saw his wife all over again.

Sweet heaven, to lose both his wife and child at the same time. The thought of such grief made her sick at heart. How does anyone deal with so much pain? She tried to put herself in his position, to imagine how she would handle anything happening to Lily, but her brain refused to make the connection, refused to even contemplate such a horror. Tears blurred her vision, and she had an overpowering need to put her arms around him.

Instead, she reached for his hand, and held it. "I'm so sorry. So very sorry."

Jared gazed into her eyes, stunned to see not only his pain reflected, but also an understanding that could only come from a kindred spirit. From someone who had survived a soul-deep hurt. She recognized his pain because she had traveled a similar path to torment. For the first time in longer than he cared to remember, he felt truly connected to another human being. Without realizing it, he covered her hand with his, holding it tightly.

"I didn't mean to blurt it out like that." The sigh he released came straight from his soul. "Seeing Donna Jean today, brought back so much . . . so many memories."

"Of course," Shannon whispered.

"I want to help. To do something for her. But she's as stubborn as Wynette. Ellis can't drive with his bad leg. What if she goes into labor alone? I tried to convince her to go into Alpine, and stay with a girlfriend of hers, but she refused. Said it was too much of an imposition. Hell, I even offered to pay for a motel room if she would go. But she's so sure that it's unnecessary. She's convinced that there won't be any problem, and it just...it just . . ."

"Terrifies you."

"Yes," he said, the word steeped in desperation.

"That's understandable considering what happened to your wife. But don't you think that for that very reason, she and her husband will be more careful? And Wynette surely will. Because of your experience they all know how quickly something can go wrong. I'm sure they've taken whatever precautions they can."

"Neal did cancel his yearly trip to the agricultural show in Odessa."

"There, you see. A precaution. And I'm sure he's taken others."

Jared looked down at her. "You're right. Neal would lay down his life for Donna Jean and that baby."

"Jared, I've only known you for a couple of days, but I know enough not to tell you to stop worrying. I have a feeling you worry about all of your friends. I also think Donna Jean knows that, and she probably worries about you. We just have to pray that everything will turn out for the best."

"I guess so. But it's hard."

"Sometimes it helps to talk about our fears. If . . . if you need to, I'll listen."

"You know about fears, don't you?"

Until that moment Shannon hadn't realized they were still holding hands. Gently, she slipped her hand from his. "What makes you ask that?"

"I saw it in your eyes a few moments ago."

"Everybody's afraid of something." She glanced away.

"I have a hunch it's more than that, but it's not my place to pry. If we knew each other better—when we know each other better—maybe I can return the favor."

"You're a kind man, Jared Markham. Your friends are lucky to have you."

"And I'm lucky you answered my ad. I didn't realize just how lucky until now."

Shannon's heart lurched in her chest. He was making it so hard to tell him she was leaving. Too hard. She couldn't do it now. Not after what had just happened.

You don't share such a profound moment with someone then turn, and say goodbye. No, she wouldn't tell him tonight. Tomorrow. She would tell him tomorrow.

"WOULD YOU CONSIDER allowing Wynette to baby-sit Lily?"

In the process of flipping a pancake, Shannon almost tossed it onto the floor. "Baby-sit?"

"Well, you haven't known any of us very long, and as a parent you have every reason to be picky about who takes care of your child. But I think Lily would enjoy seeing a working ranch, and I know Wynette would care for her as if she were her own."

"It's not that . . ."

"Then what? I always wear a beeper so there wouldn't be any problem reaching—"

"No, why?"

"Why?"

"Why would I need her to watch Lily?"

"Oh. Guess I left that part out. So we could go on a date."

"A what?"

"A date. You know, where we get dressed up. I take you out to dinner or a movie. Promise your folks I won't keep you out late, then pretend to run out of gas so we can neck."

Jared must have noticed the stricken look she couldn't stop from crossing her face. "I'm sorry. Trying to be clever was never my long suit. Should've known better."

Oh, Lord. Here she was trying to get up the nerve to tell him she was leaving, and he asks her out on a date. "No, it's not that... I didn't expect... You're asking me out on a date?"

"Absolutely. We can drive into Marathon and have dinner at the Gage Hotel, or drive into Alpine. You name it, and I'll take you."

"Oh, Jared, that's probably the nicest thing anyone has said to me in a long, long time. And I—"

The beeper, clipped to his holster, cut her off. He depressed the Recall button. "Hold that thought. I'll be right back," he said, already heading for his office.

"Oh, Jared," Shannon whispered to the empty kitchen. "I didn't know they still made men like you."

In less than five minutes he was back. "Shannon."

She was at the sink, her back to him, but the somber tone in his voice alerted her immediately. "What is it?" She turned to find him carrying a heavy jacket and duffel bag. He had the look of a man on a mission, and suddenly she was frightened. "What's wrong?"

"Can I take a rain check on our date?"

"I guess so, but—"

"Good. I'll hold you to that. There's been some trouble. DEA agents cornered a handful of Mexican nationals smuggling a controlled substance, and they need backup. Situations like this rarely last long, but these guys have a good vantage point on one of the peaks close to the park—"

"Park?"

"Big Bend National Park. About sixty miles from here." He handed her a piece of paper.

"What's this?"

"Approximately where I will be for the next eight to ten hours. Now, don't get worried. You can operate the radio like a champ. All the codes and call signs are on a sheet of paper right beside the radio. You know how to reach Wynette if you can't raise her by phone. You'll do great." He reached for his hat hanging from one of the pegs beside the kitchen door. "I hate to leave you like this, but . . ."

"You have to go." She tried to keep the alarm out of her voice, but was only moderately successful.

"Yes."

"Are there . . . The smugglers, do they have guns?"

There was no point lying to her. If they were going to make it as a couple, she would have to face the reality of his job.

"Yes. Shannon, I had hoped not to face a call like this until you felt completely comfortable with me, with...everything, but it can't be helped. I've got a job to do."

"I know." And logically she understood. What she hadn't counted on was how she would feel, seeing him headed out the door to face God knew what. She was thankful Lily was still asleep. There was no way she could pretend she wasn't scared. Lily would spot the lie before it was out of her mouth.

"If you need anything, and I mean *anything*, you call Wynette. I'll contact you as soon as I can." He was across the floor in three long strides, and yanked open the door.

"Jared?"

He turned back. This time Shannon didn't hesitate, didn't even attempt to ignore her overwhelming urge to tell him to be careful. "Take care of yourself, okay?"

He smiled. "Always. Kiss the princess for me." And then he was gone. A second later she heard the engine of his truck roar as he tore out of the driveway. And then there was silence.

She poured herself a cup of freshly brewed coffee, and sat down at the table. She needed to calm down, get her act together, she told herself. But when she lifted the mug to her lips, her hands were shaking.

Okay, so she was shaking in her slippers. This might be old hat for Jared, but it was a new experience for her. And scary didn't even begin to describe it. Easy does it, she told herself. This was his job. He probably faced similar situations on a regular basis. He was well-trained, and equipped to handle poachers, smugglers . . .

Dear Lord, they had guns.

He was going out to face men with guns. For the first time Shannon realized what Jared had meant in the copy of his ad when he stated that his life-style required a special kind of woman. He had told her that he was a law enforcement officer, but until this very minute she didn't fully comprehend what that title meant. As she sat there, images began to flash across her mind. Images of Jared and gunfire and blood.

She had to stop this. Lily would be downstairs shortly and asking for him. Shannon decided that the best thing to tell her was the truth, minus description. As if on cue, Lily padded into the kitchen.

"I'm hungry." She rubbed her eyes. "Where's Jared?"

"Well, sleepyhead, don't I rate a good morning?" Shannon brushed the bangs from her daughter's eyes.

"Good—" she yawned "—morning, Mama. Where's Jared?"

"He, uh, had to go out on a call, sweetheart."

"Can I play with the dogs?"

"May I, and yes after breakfast."

Lily nodded, and Shannon released a sigh of relief. Thank goodness she wouldn't have to lie.

And thank goodness for Mack and Pit, Shannon decided several hours later, grateful that the dogs had occupied Lily from the time her lessons were finished until lunch, then again afterward. She made a mental note to be a little more affectionate toward them as a reward for their unintentional help. Too bad she couldn't find something to occupy her mind so easily. She had tried twice to raise Jared by radio, and got no response. She was tempted to keep trying, but didn't for fear she might be preventing an important transmission. As the day wore on without any word from him, her nerves frayed like an old worn rug.

Late in the afternoon, using the excuse of checking on Donna Jean, Shannon called the Dickerson ranch. But her heart sank when it became clear that Wynette wasn't even aware Jared was gone, much less on an urgent call. By the time she ended the conversation, Shannon was even more worried.

Why hadn't he called?

Every time the question popped into her mind, she got an answer she didn't like. She had read somewhere that there was an extremely high rate of alcoholism among policemen's wives, and a sixty percent divorce rate. No wonder. How did a woman wait like this day in and day out without going a little crazy?

Just look at her. She had practically spent the entire day listening for a message over the radio or by phone. And here she was again sitting beside the phone, waiting, hoping, praying it would ring, and Jared would be on the other end.

Earlier she had been so worried about Lily bonding with Jared that she hadn't stopped to think about how she might feel if anything happened to him. Now look what had happened. She had done the very thing she knew she shouldn't. She cared about Jared. Maybe too much.

The day crawled by like a tired snake, and as dusk turned to darkness, Shannon was worn down to her last nerve. To her credit, she kept up a reasonable amount of chatter, and enough of a poker face to keep Lily from getting suspicious. And if the child noticed that her mother carried the handheld mobile radio everywhere they went, she didn't mention it.

"I wanna kiss Jared good-night," Lily said as Shannon tucked her in bed.

"Well, sweetheart he's still working."

"When's he gonna be here?"

"I'm sure he'll be back as soon as he can." Shannon kept her voice calm, despite the fact that her insides were jumping like cold water on a hot griddle.

"I can wait 'til he—" Lily yawned twice "—comes home."

"Nice try, slugger, but I don't think you'll make it. How about if I tell Jared to come up and see you, even if you're already asleep?"

"Promise?"

"Promise," Shannon whispered, hoping it was one she wouldn't have to break. When she leaned over to kiss Lily's cheek, two heavy little eyelids were barely open.

"Night, Mama." The last word trailed off and within moments, Lily was sound asleep.

"Good night, my angel."

Two hours later when Shannon peeked in on Lily she envied the way her child slept on, blissfully unaware of what was happening. Not that she actually had any better idea than Lily about what was going on. All that she knew was that Jared was somewhere out there in the mountains. In the dark. With guns. Twelve hours, and still no message on the radio. The phone was deathly quiet.

"Stay busy. Idle minds are the devil's playground, or something like that. Just don't—dwell on—the bad stuff."

Heeding her own advice, she made a grocery list. Then she read a couple of curriculum catalogs for some courses she wanted for Lily. After that she went upstairs and dug out a piece of unfinished cross-stitch she had been dragging around for months, but she couldn't concentrate. Finally, she found a novel on one of Jared's bookshelves that looked interesting. Sitting at the kitchen table so that she would hear him the instant he drove up, she started chapter one. A half hour later, after she had read the first page twice and couldn't remember one word, she gave up.

And all the while the mobile radio sat within easy reach, quiet except for static or the occasional voice of a rancher jumping from channel to channel looking for a chat. Despite the fact that she was unbelievably tired, she kept staring at it as if she could will Jared's voice to interrupt the static with the message "Shannon, I'm coming home. Shannon . . ."

"Shannon."

Jared was calling her, but from far away. Slowly she lifted her head from the table where she had fallen asleep. "Jared?"

"Shannon, do you copy?" he said over the radio.

She snatched it up, holding it in front of her face as if she could see him. "Jared? Jared, where are you?"

"Shannon." A pause, then, "This is Markham, out."

"No, Jared. Wait!"

Why couldn't he hear her? Oh, she hadn't pushed the damned button to transmit. She was fumbling to hit the right button when she heard the faint sound of an engine. It grew louder, and louder.

He was home!

Shannon plunked the radio down on the table none too gently and jumped up from the chair. She wanted to throw open the door and rush outside to meet him, but thought better of it. Besides, he would probably think she was a hysterical female if he knew how frantic she had been.

The dogs whined and pranced in anticipation as he approached, and Shannon knew exactly how they felt. Her heart was racing like a bullet train.

She heard the door to his truck slam shut, then his footsteps on the porch. He unlocked the back door and stepped inside, duffel bag under one arm, jacket under the other.

He came to a screeching halt when he saw her. "Shannon? I saw the lights, but I never expected you to be awake."

Dreamed, hoped, he thought, but certainly not expected. She looked like an angel in her white robe and slippers, her hair unbraided and tumbling over her shoulders. He wanted to haul her into his arms and kiss her so bad he ached, but he was afraid she wasn't ready.

His uniform was dusty and dirty. He looked exhausted. And absolutely wonderful. "I...I waited..."

"You didn't have to, but I'm glad you did."

Suddenly Shannon couldn't stand being so far—a whole eight feet—away from him. It was almost as if she had to make sure he was real. She crossed to him. "Are you...are you all right?"

"For the most part."

"You're not hurt? I thought... I was afraid you were..."

"I'm dead tired, starved and filthy, but other than—"

"Thank God," she whispered, her eyes filled with tears. Without thinking about his reaction or the consequences, she put her arms around him, and lay her head on his chest.

The duffel bag and jacket hit the floor with a thump. Jared's arms found much softer cargo. He held her to him, stroking her back, grateful for this much, at least. "It's all right. I'm all right."

"You didn't call. Hours went by, and I was so worried."

He held her tighter. "I'm so sorry, Shannon. Everything happened so fast. We had to track the perps over some rough terrain. When you're in the moment like that, you have to stay focused on the job. And I— Well, it's been so long since I've had someone waiting for me to call."

At that moment being his "someone" sounded like the most wonderful thing in the world, despite its obvious drawbacks. At that moment she couldn't imagine anything more important than being here, in his arms. She wanted him to kiss her. Wanted to kiss him back.

"Crazy as it sounds considering the circumstances, it feels good."

His words snapped her back to reality as nothing else could. She was in his arms, and loving it, and a heartbeat away from kissing him. And then how could she tell him she wouldn't be here the next time he needed someone to be waiting? No, a kiss was too much. Kissing Jared would be too dangerous, too...thrilling. She *had* to distance herself, and that was all there was to it.

"You mean you forgot about us?" she said with a sniff.

"No!" He pulled away to look at her. "Oh, God, no, but—"

"It's all right, Jared." She offered him a tiny smile. "I was only teasing you a little. Besides, I'm so glad you're safe it doesn't really matter." Then with a loosely doubled fist she gave his chest a weak rap. "Where have you been, anyway? Do you have any idea how long it's been since I saw you walk out that door?"

Relief rushed though Jared's body like a spring flood out of the mountains. Enough to enable him to smile back. If she had enough spunk to demand explanations, she was over the worst of her fear. In the hours since leaving her, he had done his fair share of worrying. He didn't know how she would handle the stress his job generated, and the thought that she might not be able to handle it at all terrified him. Thank heaven, she had kept her cool, and found a way to cope. She was as remarkable as she was beautiful.

"Get dish-slinging mad if it will help."

She sniffed again. "Only if I can throw them at you."

"We can probably work something out with paper plates."

Shannon sighed, torn between relief and regret. "No good. Not enough noise."

"Feel better?"

She nodded. "You mentioned starved. How does a meat-loaf sandwich sound to you?"

"Like a gourmet meal. Got enough for two? My belly is rubbing my backbone."

"I think I can swing that."

"Great. I'll go wash up." At the doorway he stopped abruptly, and turned to face her. He stared at her for a long moment. So long Shannon became uncomfortable.

Then he walked straight back, and did what he had been wanting to do since the minute he found her waiting up for him. He took her in his arms and kissed her.

And kissed her.

Later Shannon would question why she didn't flinch when he hauled her into his arms. Later she would question why she hadn't pulled away. For now, the only thought in her brain was, yes, yes, yes.

He fitted his mouth to hers, tasting, but not testing. There was nothing tentative about the way he applied just enough pressure so that her lips parted and warmed. There was no hesitation as he took the kiss deeper. His need was obvious.

What surprised her was her own need. She leaned into him, lifting her hands to the back of his head and gave herself fully to the whirlwind of sensations storming her body. His taste was dark, male, and shot straight to her center like a flash of lightning. When he pulled away, she wanted to pull him back.

"Shannon." Her gaze met his. "I'm sorry I didn't call, but I couldn't. It tore me up knowing you were waiting without any word. It's not fair. It's hard as hell on a woman. But it is my job. It's also part of who I am. I want you to stay." His forehead touched hers. "God, but I want you to stay." Then he drew back.

"But if you can't handle my job—the stress—I'll understand. No one, least of all me, will blame you for leaving."

He was giving her an out.

The very thing she thought she wanted. All she had to do was take it. She and Lily could walk out the door. Move on. Keep running. Eventually, hopefully, she would find a way to shake Hal. They would survive. Jared would survive.

Eventually, she might even be able to convince herself that he wasn't the kindest man she had ever met. Or the gentlest. She might even talk herself into believing that she didn't care. That his kiss had meant nothing.

All she had to do was speak up, and she was out, gone. Free and clear. She could do it. It was what she had planned. And it was probably the best thing for everybody. While her mind agreed, her heart hesitated. She couldn't even use Lily as an excuse anymore.

This wasn't about Lily. It was about her. And Jared. And the truth, whether she liked it or not, was that she wanted to stay. Call it wishful thinking, call it absolute, total insanity, but she wanted to stay. While an insistent voice inside her head urged caution, the stronger voice of her heart whispered, take a chance.

"I—I waited, didn't I?"

Once the words were out of her mouth, Shannon felt as if an enormous weight had been lifted from her shoulders. She had made her decision, and prayed it was the right one for all of them.

"Yes." He cupped her face and kissed her again, this time briefly, then stepped away. "You won't be sorry," he promised. Then he went upstairs, leaving Shannon staring after him.

In the blink of an eye, more specifically with one kiss, everything had changed. She was in serious danger of getting in way over her head with this man, of wanting too much. And far too close to losing her heart.

6

"HOW WOULD YOU two beautiful ladies like to go on a picnic?"

Shannon and Lily glanced up from their reading lesson. "A picnic? Where, where? I wanna go," Lily said excitedly.

"If it's okay with your mother, we can go for a drive along a road called the El Camino del Rio. That's Spanish for The River Road, and it's some of the prettiest country in Texas. It takes most of the day, so we'll have to pack a lunch."

"Don't you have to work today?" Shannon asked.

"Tomorrow is my regular day off, but I traded with Tucker. He was supposed to pick up some paperwork at the state park. Instead, I'll do that, then the rest of the day is ours. I thought you might like to get out of the house."

Three days had passed since their kiss. Three days of wondering if it would happen again, and what she would do if it did. They had gotten to know each other a little better in that time, at least on the surface. They had talked about his job and Lily's schooling. Discussed the weather, and the upcoming Thanksgiving holiday. They had talked about almost everything but the kiss.

And it was driving Shannon crazy. She couldn't think about anything else. An outing might be just the thing to distract her.

She smiled. "We're out of potato chips. How am I going to pack a lunch without potato chips?"

"We'll just have to stop on the way. No self-respecting picnic would be caught dead without potato chips."

"Yippee!" Lily jumped out of her chair, and ran to Jared.

He scooped her up into his arms, and gave one of her braids a playful yank. "Let's see now. I may need someone to help me navigate."

"Me! Me!"

"Can you read a map?"

"I can read *The Spooky Old Tree* all by myself."

"Good enough. I hereby dub you my official navigator." He sat her on her feet.

"Yippee! Mama can help, too."

Jared's gaze met Shannon's. "Of course she can. It wouldn't be any fun without her."

Shannon closed the reader, and stacked it on top of Lily's other books. "Then we better get busy."

Jared watched them walk hand in hand toward the kitchen, and wondered if he hadn't lost what was left of his mind. Three days, and Shannon hadn't uttered one word about the kiss they had shared. Of course, he hadn't exactly been a chatterbox on the subject, either.

He wanted to give her time to get used to him, used to thinking of him in more romantic terms. But three days of being with her, listening to her laugh and sing to Lily, three days of remembering the way she felt in his arms, the way she tasted, was driving him crazy.

Yeah, the picnic was a good idea. He needed the distraction.

Thirty minutes later Jared was loading the cooler filled with sandwiches and soft drinks into the back of the truck when Shannon stuck her head out of the back door and yelled, "Jared, come quick!"

He raced into the house. Shannon was in the kitchen, the telephone receiver in her hand. "What's wrong?"

"It's Ellis. He says Wynette is at the café. Neal is out somewhere on the ranch working with a couple of the hands. And Donna Jean is in labor."

Jared paled. "Oh, God." He took the phone from Shannon. "Yeah, Ellis. I know, but you need to stay calm. Did you get Neal on the CB? Well, how long ago did he check in? Another hour? Damn!" He looked at Shannon. "I'm on my way."

"And we're going with you," she said as soon as he hung up the phone.

"You sure?"

"I didn't find Lily under a cabbage leaf. I might be able to help."

"Okay, get Lily, and I'll meet you at the truck." He headed for the back door, then stopped. "Sorry about our picnic," he said.

"New babies beat picnics hands down."

They were in the truck and racing toward the Dickerson ranch in short order. "Will the new baby be there at Wynette's house?" Lily wanted to know.

Jared and Shannon looked at each other over the top of Lily's head. "I hope not. No, I don't think so, sweetheart."

"When can I see it?"

"Maybe soon. But you may have to wait. Sometimes babies think they want to be born, but then they change their minds, and wait awhile."

"Did I do that?"

"Nope. You were in a hurry." Shannon prayed Donna Jean's baby didn't come as quickly as Lily had. Hal had barely reached the hospital in time.

It took hardly more than fifteen minutes to reach the Dickerson house. Ellis was standing on the front porch looking terrified and clutching his cane like a life preserver.

Jared made hasty introductions. "Ellis Dickerson, Shannon Kramer, and her daughter, Lily."

"Howdy, ma'am." His eyes were a little wild looking, and she wasn't certain he even saw them.

"Hello," Lily said. "Did the baby hurry?"

Shannon patted Lily's shoulder. "Not now, sweetheart."

"But, Mama—"

"She's in pain," Ellis told Jared. "We've got to do something."

"Did you call Wynette?"

"Told her you were coming, and we'd be there soon as we could. She's gonna meet us at the hospital."

"Okay, I'll put Donna Jean in your station wagon," he told Ellis.

His voice was steady, and he appeared in control, but Shannon knew he must be tied in knots. "Shannon, can you follow me in my truck with Ellis?"

"Of course."

"What about Neal?" Ellis Dickerson was near panic.

"We'll worry about Neal later." Jared reached for the front door.

Shannon put a hand on his arm. "Jared, why don't you let me go in to check on Donna Jean? We may all be rushing around unnecessarily."

"Oh," he said. "Yeah."

"First bedroom on the right," Ellis told her.

"Lily, wait here with Jared, and I'll be right back."

Ten minutes later Shannon, carrying an overnight case, emerged from the bedroom, her arm around Donna Jean's ample waist.

"You took time to pack!" Jared couldn't believe his eyes.

"Hi." Donna Jean gave him a weak smile.

"I don't believe this—"

"Jared, we need to get to the hospital as quickly as possible, but we don't need to break any speed records. This baby is determined to arrive today, but we do have a little time."

"I'm fine. Really," Donna Jean assured them. "Daddy, will you get Neal—" A contraction cut short her sentence. She clutched her stomach and groaned. Both men blanched.

"We'll find Neal," Shannon promised.

"To hell with Neal." Jared swept Donna Jean into his arms, and headed for the garage.

The entire situation might have been comical if Jared wasn't scared right down to his toes. But he was in no mood to see any humor in what was happening. Shannon was certainly no expert, but Donna Jean's pains were twenty minutes apart, and the hospital was less than an hour away. They should be able to make it with plenty of time to spare.

If Jared didn't go to pieces first.

In fact, the more Shannon thought about it, the more she was convinced that perhaps she should be the one to drive Donna Jean. She started walking toward the garage, but Jared already had his passenger ensconced in the back seat, and the station wagon backed out.

"Jared." She put her hands on the car, and ducked her head to be able to see his face. "Jared, I think I should go with you."

"But—but, Ellis and Neal—"

"Can come along as soon as Ellis reaches Neal. But I think Donna Jean might be more comfortable if she had another woman along."

"Oh, please." Donna Jean was obviously relieved. "Shannon, I would be so grateful."

"But there's no time—"

She touched Jared's arm. "It will be all right." As quickly as she could, she buckled Lily in the front seat with Jared, praying her presence would be a reminder not to take unnecessary risks. Then Shannon scrambled into the back seat.

She knew Jared wouldn't endanger Donna Jean or her baby, but she also knew he was frantic not to let history repeat itself. She said a quick prayer for all of them—and every other driver on the road between here and the hospital.

They had no sooner pulled out of the gravel driveway and onto the main road leading into Alpine when Donna Jean had another contraction. After it had passed, both women looked at each other, knowing it had barely been fifteen minutes since the last one.

"Is she okay?" Jared asked.

Shannon glanced at her watch. "She's fine. You just concentrate on driving."

Donna Jean clutched her hand. "But—"

"Shh. You're going to be fine, and so is your baby. Now, have you and Neal been to any Lamaze classes?"

"Four times—at the—hospital."

"And you learned how to focus and breathe?"

"Yes."

"That's good. Very good. When you feel a contraction coming I want you to breathe the way they taught you. And focus." Shannon glanced around the back seat of the station wagon in search of something to use as a focal point, and came up empty-handed. "Jared, give me your badge."

"My what?"

"Give me your badge to use as a focal point."

"A focal—"

"Just give me the damned badge," she snapped.

"Mama," Lily's eyes rounded, hearing her mother's profanity. "You're not supposed to—"

"I'm sorry, sweetheart," she said, as Jared all but ripped the emblem of authority from his shirt, and handed it to her.

"Okay." She held up the shiny metal badge. "Here's our focus."

"Maybe you should get her to lie down."

Shannon understood Jared's need to be helpful, but at the moment she could do without it.

"She can't be very comfortable—"

"I'm fine, Jared, really—" Donna Jean groaned, in the grip of another contraction.

"Focus," Shannon ordered. "And breathe." They breathed together until it passed.

The commotion in the back seat sounded too intense not to be urgent. "My God, Shannon. What if we don't make it?" Jared uttered.

She put her hand on his shoulder. "You're doing great." But his white-knuckled grip on the steering wheel testified to the fact that he was scared to death. "We'll get there in time, Jared. This time everything will turn out all right."

Her voice was so calm, her words so caring, they took the edge off his fear. She knew exactly what he needed to hear at that very moment. Jared wanted to reach up and hold her hand, but he didn't dare take a hand off the steering wheel. But when this was over . . .

"SO, HOW DOES IT FEEL to be a godfather?"

"Is he supposed to be that color?" Jared asked without taking his eyes off the wiggling bundle wrapped in blue on the other side of the nursery window.

Shannon smiled at the intense expression on his face. "Yes."

"You're sure?"

"Absolutely. Lily looked like a little red-faced tomato until she was about two days old."

Jared shot her a disbelieving look. "Really?"

"Cross my heart. In a week young Joshua Jared Hartley will be pink as a rosebud. The only time he'll get red in the face is when he demands to be fed, and doesn't get an immediate response."

"I wish they hadn't stuck him with a name like Joshua *Jared*."

The big, broad-shouldered game warden had actually looked on the verge of tears when Neal came out of the delivery room and announced they had named their baby for Donna Jean's favorite biblical character and her best friend.

"It's a compliment."

"Yeah? He might not think so."

"My guess is that once he gets to know you, he'll be flattered."

They stood gazing at the baby for several moments, content to enjoy the wonder of viewing a miracle.

"Where's Lily?"

"She and Wynette are in the gift shop buying something for the baby."

"But he's only two hours old."

"Spending money on grandchildren is part of a woman's genetic code. I think it's in our DNA or something."

"That reminds me. I need to buy the baby—"

"Joshua."

"I need to buy Joshua a gift. Would you...would you go with me?"

She gazed up at him. "I'd love to. Besides, you'd probably come home with a bicycle or his first pair of boots."

Jared grinned. He liked the sound of the word home on her lips. It felt right. "Not appropriate, huh?"

"In about five years, maybe."

"So, we're talking blankets and diapers." He wrinkled his nose. "Baby stuff?"

"You know, you could do something different."

"Like?"

"A savings bond, or starting a savings account in Joshua's name. If you decide on a savings account, then Wynette and Ellis, or Neal's family could add to it over the years. But then, bonds are—" She glanced up, and found him looking at her strangely. "What? It was just a suggestion. You don't—"

"I haven't thanked you."

"For what? All I did was hold Donna Jean's hand, and remind her to breathe."

"You did much more than that. You were nothing short of a heroine. She should have named the baby after you."

"I hardly think—"

"Seriously. You were great. Calm, steady. Just what she needed."

"I was glad I could help."

"And you were just what I needed." He reached for her hand. "You saved me today, Shannon. I was scared spitless that something bad was going to happen. Just like with Amy. Having you there, knowing you understood was the only thing that got me through it. I'm not much on pretty words, but thank you." He took her face in his hands and kissed her.

She tasted like warm honey and wine, and the taste went straight to his head. The feel of her body against his was a powerful reminder of the hours, days he had thought of nothing else but this. He had intended the kiss to be an expression of his gratitude, but it didn't take long before it became something else entirely. Something hotter. He held her close, his hands molding her to him. Totally lost in the kiss, the sound of an elevator door opening penetrated his consciousness enough to remind him they were in a public place.

Breathless, dazed and definitely aroused, Shannon was grateful to see Lily and Wynette step off the elevator. While her daughter chattered on about every item of baby paraphernalia in the entire gift shop, Shannon kept stealing glances at Jared.

If she wasn't careful she could fall for him in a big way. She was honest enough with herself to admit she wanted him, but it was more than sex. So, where did that leave her? This had started out as a temporary stop on a journey to a new life, but what if this *became* the new life?

Shannon called herself ten times a fool. There was nothing wrong with fantasies, unless they started to take over reality. And she couldn't allow herself the luxury of believing in happy endings. Could she?

"SORRY ABOUT the picnic," Jared said as they drove home. "And that drive down south along the El Camino del Rio."

"You're off the hook so long as I get a rain check."

"Promise."

"Okay, I'll hold you to it." Lily was asleep, her head in Shannon's lap. She brushed a lock of hair from her daughter's forehead. "You must admit, the day was exciting."

"No question about that."

"And exhausting."

"You tired?"

"Funny, I wouldn't have said so until the last few minutes, but yes. Particularly since I know what the first question out of my daughter's mouth will be bright and early tomorrow morning."

"When can she go see little Joshua?"

"Bingo. She wanted to bring him home with us."

Jared laughed. "I'm sure she'll be welcome at the Dickerson ranch as often as she wants to go. That reminds me. You owe me a date."

"What?"

"A date, remember? We talked about it right before I got the call for the DEA assist."

"Oh, yeah."

"Unless you've changed your mind."

She was surprised at how quickly the denial sprang from her lips. "No."

"About the date, or about staying."

"What makes you say that?"

"You know, when you waited and worried about me the other night, I was thrilled. It made me feel . . . well, closer to you. But I realize that we've never really discussed how my job might affect you and Lily. For instance, I've noticed that you don't seem the least bit uncomfortable with the fact that I wear a gun all the time. Even when I'm off duty."

"I . . . no. I grew up around guns. All of my brothers learned to shoot while they were still in grade school."

"How many brothers have you got?"

"Seven."

"Seven? None of them live close by with shotguns, I hope."

Shannon laughed. "They're all back in West Virginia."

"That's where you're from, I take it."

For a second the questions pushed her panic button, and she had to remind herself this was Jared asking. He had no ulterior motives. Still, months of evading such questions were hard to forget. "Originally. But I haven't lived there in a long time."

"Your family still there?"

"Scattered. One in the Navy. A couple married. One in college in Charleston. One working in Pittsburgh. The rest, God knows where." Talking about her brothers was a bittersweet reminder of all she had given up. All Hal had cost her. But, if not seeing her brothers for years meant keeping Lily out of Hal's reach, it was worth it.

"So, you're not close to them?"

"No, not since my divorce." The words were hardly out of her mouth before she realized it was an opening to a subject she didn't want to talk about. Of course, Jared had no way of knowing that.

"Is your ex-husband still in West Virginia?"

"He...he died not too long after we were divorced."

"Oh, I'm sorry."

"I'm not."

At the coldness in her voice Jared shot her a quick look. "Did he hurt you or Lily?"

Shannon almost laughed out loud. He couldn't know, must never know how close he had come to the truth. "He wasn't one tenth the man you are. Not as a friend or a father."

"Shannon—"

"Oh, good," she said hoping to distract him. "We're home."

Jared parked the truck, and carried Lily into the house, then upstairs to bed. He was on the front porch in a bench swing when Shannon joined him.

She sat down beside him, wrapping her arms around herself.

"Cold?"

Gazing at the sky, she shook her head. "Goose bumps. Look at those stars. You never see them like this in the city."

"Too many artificial lights."

"The city's loss. It's wonderful," she whispered.

"Hmm."

They swung silently for a while, content to savor the soft star-filled night. Shannon found herself leaning toward him until finally her head was on his shoulder. Jared held her close.

"Do you realize that you and Lily have been here a whole week?" he said finally.

"Seems longer."

"Is that good or bad?"

"Good. Comfortable."

"Yeah, for me, too."

After a long silence, Jared said, "You know, you were right about me from the beginning. I am lonely. Or I was until you came along. Shannon, I . . ." He leaned forward to look into her eyes but they were closed. Her chest rose and fell with the even rhythm of sleep.

Gently, ever so gently, he lifted her until she was cradled in his lap like a child. Then he rose, his well-muscled body barely straining under her slight weight, and carried her inside, upstairs, and placed her beside Lily on the bed. He covered her with a quilt.

And then he simply watched the two of them sleep.

The two princesses that had come into his life. Lily had already won his heart, and now he realized her mother had, too.

He hadn't intended to fall in love. Until today he had felt guilty merely thinking about loving someone other than Amy. His guilt about not being there when Amy needed him, and his fear that it might happen again were all tangled up together, and had a choke hold on his emotions, on his life. The instant Shannon had put her hand on his shoulder and said, "This time everything will turn out all right," he had felt that it truly would.

Watching Shannon's quiet strength had made him see that he had never confronted his fear, and had allowed it to isolate him from living life as it should be. He would always have a place in his heart for Amy, and he would always grieve his unborn son, but that didn't mean he couldn't make a place in his heart for someone else. For these two females who'd come along and changed him.

And the thought that he had almost walked away from them made him tremble.

Fate, he thought, sure had a strange way of bringing people together. A week ago, he had felt sorry for Shannon Kramer, and her freckle-faced little girl, and now...

Now he was in love with both of them.

The only obstacle he could see was Shannon herself. Or, more appropriately, whatever she was afraid of. From the beginning, he had sensed that trusting someone didn't come easy to her. After the way she had changed the subject tonight, he had a good idea where her fear might have originated. Her ex-husband. Had he abused Shannon? Maybe Lily as well?

The thought made him sick to his stomach. He broke out in a cold sweat. It was a good thing the man was dead, because if he had hurt them and was still alive, Jared would have been tempted to go after the bastard himself.

Softly, he walked to Shannon's side of the bed, and bent down until his face was close to hers. He would teach her to trust him. To trust what they could have together. He already knew she was a passionate woman. All she needed was the freedom to express her passion with a man she trusted. Jared intended to be that man.

GAZING OUT the kitchen window at a field of wild flowers on the edge of Jared's property with the mountains in the background, Shannon found it hard to believe that she had ever thought of this country as barren or desolate. It was majestic with an unadorned grandeur that could take your breath away at times. Last night's sunset was one of those times.

Lily and the dogs had been playing in the backyard while Jared grilled hamburgers. She had brought them both a soft drink, and stayed to watch the sun gasp its last breath of the day, expiring in a blaze of golden glory. And Jared had kissed her.

Come to think of it, there had been a lot of that going on lately. Ever since the night Joshua was born. In fact, she had begun to think he was waging an all-out, one-man war on her senses. Not a day went by that he didn't find an opportunity to touch her. And it was more than a casual peck on the cheek as he left in the morning, or an occasional arm draped companionably about her shoulders.

There was nothing casual or companionable about the hundreds of very creative ways he found to be near her, to touch her.

For instance, the other day, he'd been playfully teasing Lily by pretending to whisper a secret in Shannon's ear. And while he whispered nonsense his lips skimmed along the rim of her ear, and sent sensual currents shooting through her nerves like live wire in an electrical storm. He was short-circuiting her willpower, and he knew it.

Then, the night afterward, when they had all been cleaning up the kitchen, some 40's big band era music started playing on the radio. Jared had asked Lily to dance. With her little stocking feet on top of his massive boots, they had waltzed around the floor, the five-year-old alternating between giggling and gazing adoringly at Jared. Then in one quick, smooth move, he changed partners. He overrode Shannon's weak protests, and before she knew it, they were swaying to Glen Miller's "Moonlight Serenade." Quickly forgoing the traditional hold he lifted her arms to encircle his neck. His hands went to the small of her back, then slipped slightly lower to the curve of her hips. He pressed her to him ever so gently.

Shannon almost gasped at the contact. Every nerve, every cell in her body responded in the most elemental way. When his hand coasted up her back and pressed again, she could feel her nipples harden against his chest. Her throat went desert dry, and she almost stumbled. By the end of the dance she was tingling from head to toe.

And then, there was the time he had caught her massaging the muscles in her neck, and insisted on taking over the task, his big hands gently kneading. Then he made her lie down on her stomach on the sofa so—according to him—he could do it properly. What began as an effort to relax her backfired. Big time.

Jared worked the tendons across her shoulder blades, down her spine to her waist. His fingers kneaded the muscles from the small of her back, around to her rib cage. And each time his hands lightly brushed the sides of her breasts. The first time she hadn't been able to prevent a betraying hitch in her breath. The second time she had clamped her teeth together, but by the fourth and fifth strokes, a soft moan slipped from between her lips. She lay beneath his powerful hands, her body languid from the massage and aroused from his "accidental" touches.

But the final straw, the pièce de résistance of his sensual assault had been the ice cream. Plain old vanilla ice cream.

One afternoon after dusting off Jared's electric ice cream freezer, and searching through the cookbooks at her disposal, Shannon had succeeded in preparing a gallon and a half of rich vanilla frozen custard. She was just removing the dasher as Jared came inside after stacking some firewood in a rack alongside the house. He was wearing jeans and a T-shirt and she was impressed all over again by his size and build.

Naturally, he asked for a taste.

She spooned some of the cream into his mouth. Watching him lick his lips, her stomach did a couple of somersaults. Then he had returned the favor by offering her a spoonful of the cool confection. Thinking back, she was certain that he had deliberately left a drop or two on her lips so that he could kiss it off. And, oh, but he had done a wonderful job.

First his tongue coasted slowly over her lower lip. Once, twice as he collected the dot of sweet vanilla. He drew back just far enough to look into her eyes as he licked his lips again. Those faultless blue eyes sparked with desire as he watched her. Long seconds. Enough time for her to turn away. When she didn't, he fitted his mouth to hers and kissed her deeply. The lingering sweetness of the ice cream mingled with desire was like ambrosia, and went to her head like too much wine. If Wynette hadn't picked that moment to stop by with a share of the harvest from her garden, Shannon wasn't sure where all that heat would have taken them. No, that wasn't true. She knew.

Shannon shivered with the memory. She sighed. Even now gazing out at the wildflowers, she could still hear her own voice, husky with need as she called his name. But as well as she remembered the heat they generated, she also remembered that on each occasion he had never pressed her to go any further than she wanted to go. Each time—during the dance, the massage and the ice cream tasting—he had given her plenty of opportunities to walk away or to tell him to stop. He let her call the shots. And instinctively Shannon knew that, had she protested at all, he would have stopped. He had given her that power. The fact that she had repeatedly chosen not to exercise it was more a testimony to his patience than her willpower.

And his campaign was still going on. It was almost as if once he had discovered how to turn her on, he couldn't resist doing it. Every day, in every way, he made certain she was aware that he wanted her. More important he made certain she was aware that she wanted him. She couldn't even escape him in her dreams. Night after night she had the most erotic dreams. Several times she had awakened in the dark to find she was clutching the sheets, her skin damp with perspiration. She wasn't sure how much more she could take.

The torture was sweet.

It was hot.

And it was driving her crazy.

Maybe it was a good thing Jared was going to be out in the hills most of the night. Even though she worried, it gave her a much needed opportunity to do some serious thinking. And to ask herself some very important questions.

Like, how was she going to tell a man that placed a premium on honesty that she had lied to him? And in the next breath tell him that she was falling in love with him?

THE QUESTIONS were still unanswered as Shannon and
Lily drove to the Dickerson ranch to visit Donna Jean
and the baby. Disappointed to find the baby asleep
when they arrived, Lily had gladly accepted Ellis's offer of a pony ride as a consolation prize. Shannon,
Donna Jean and Wynette sipped iced tea, and talked
about what each was preparing for the Thanksgiving
dinner they would be sharing, as well as how best to
schedule dinner around the trillions of football games
the men always wanted to watch.

Shannon kept peeking into the cradle, checking to see
if Josh was awake. She peeked so often that she finally
woke him herself.

"He's awake," she announced with a sly grin. "Can
I pick him up?"

"Might as well," Wynette said. "You been working
on it for the last fifteen minutes."

Laughing, Shannon scooped little Josh into her arms.
"Look at this. Not even a whimper. He's such a good
baby."

"For the most part." Wynette had cut back on her
hours at the café, and the reason was clear. She couldn't
stop smiling around her grandson. "Might argue that
point around three in the mornin' when his belly gets
empty."

Donna Jean rolled her eyes. "As if he cried for more
than two seconds with you around. I'll bet you didn't
jump and run every time I made a peep."

"Hey, that's one of the perks of bein' a grandmother. You get to pick 'em up any time you want to, then when they start to cry you get to hand 'em back to their mama."

Shannon held the baby high in her arms. "You don't cry, do you Joshua? No, sir. Why, you're an angel, aren't you? And such a handsome boy," she cooed. Gazing at the sweet face of this beautiful child, her heart turned over. For half a second, just a heartbeat, she thought about holding a child of her own—hers and Jared's. "Oh, sweet baby," she whispered. "What a lovely dream you are."

Donna Jean and Wynette exchanged glances.

"Don't you think Shannon looks real natural with a baby in her arms, Mama?"

"No doubt about it," Wynette concurred.

"And a little brother for Lily would be nice to kinda round things out, don't you think?"

"No argument there. You know, I bet if she put her mind to it, among other things, I figure she could be holdin' her own baby in say, ten or eleven months from now."

Shannon nuzzled Josh's baby-powder-scented cheek. "You two are not exactly subtle." The baby began to root at her breast. "You either." She kissed the top of his downy head.

"We were hopin' you'd get the message." Donna Jean relieved her of Josh who had now began to fuss. "And I'm about to get a loud message from my son."

While Donna Jean took the baby into the nursery to change and feed him, Wynette fetched more iced tea. Lily arrived, ecstatic to learn Josh was awake, and dashed inside to the nursery. Shannon smiled at the excitement in her daughter's voice.

"She's pretty crazy about that baby," Wynette said.

"If she had her way, we'd be over here every day."

"Wouldn't bother us. You're family."

Shannon looked over at her friend. "That's nice. Thanks."

"You know, Donna Jean and I were serious a while ago. You do make a pretty picture holdin' a baby. And unless I miss my guess, you got a man dyin' to make that picture a reality." Wynette set her glass of tea aside, and leaned forward. "He's gone on you. Gone as gone can get."

"I . . . I don't know what to say."

"Don't have to say a thing. The way you looked at little Josh just about says it all. Admit it, Shannon. You were lookin' at Josh, but you were thinkin' about holdin' Jared's baby."

Shannon opened her mouth to protest, then closed it.

"Just what I thought. Does Jared know you're as crazy about him as he is about you?"

"Did . . . did he tell you that he was in love with me?"

"Didn't have to. It's there for any fool to see every time he looks at you. What I want to know, is what you're going to do about it."

"I—I'm not sure," Shannon answered honestly.

"Listen, sugar, I know you had good reasons for buyin' a pig in a poke, so to speak. And I always got the impression there was somethin' in your past you'd just as soon not talk about."

"What makes you say that?"

"Call it a hunch. The point is, no matter how this thing between you and Jared got started, or what you left behind, I'm tellin' you straight out that now you got yourself a good man, an honest man. He'll love and cherish you and that darlin' Lily 'til the end of your days, if you'll give him the chance."

Wynette had just described Shannon's dream of a lifetime. If she only knew, Shannon thought. If she only knew....

At that moment Donna Jean and Lily came back into the room. "One baby, full, burped and dry. Thanks to my assistant."

Lily beamed. "Mama, can we get a baby like Josh?"

Wynette's gaze met Shannon's. "Out of the mouths of babes."

"I can take good care of him. Donna Jean says so. Can we, Mama?"

"May we, and we'll talk about it later. Now, it's time we headed for home."

"Y'all don't need to run off," Donna Jean said. "Why don't you stay for supper?"

"Thanks, but we should—"

"You ask your Mama about the calf?" Ellis asked, joining them.

Lily jumped out of her chair. "I forgot. Mama, Ellis said I could see the baby calf when it gets borned." She turned pleading eyes to her mother. "Please?"

"What calf?"

"Got a cow that's due to calf any minute," Ellis explained. "And I told Lily she could stay and see the newborn if it was all right with you."

Being raised in West Virginia, Shannon had seen more farm animals give birth than she could count, and knew that most turned out fine. But occasionally a delivery might go bad, and she didn't want Lily witnessing a stillbirth. "After the birth, right?"

"Oh, sure," Ellis said.

Wynette grinned. "Seems like babies are poppin' up all over the place."

Shannon cut her a glance, then redirected her attention to Lily. "I suppose we could— Oh, no. I forgot that I've got two loaves of bread rising. I'm sorry, sweetheart, but we have to go home."

"Neal can bring her home after supper," Ellis offered. "Be no trouble."

"I got a better idea," Wynette said, still grinning. "Why don't you let Lily stay over?"

"Oh, I couldn't—"

"Sure you could. She'll be fine."

"But what about pajamas?"

"She can use one of Neal's T-shirts for a gown, and she can sleep on the sofa bed," Donna Jean suggested. "It would give you some time to yourself."

"Jared's gonna be out most of the night. Take a bubble bath. Do your nails. Read a book."

Shannon sighed. "Sounds like heaven."

Ellis frowned. "Not afraid to stay by yourself, are you?"

"No, not at all. But I hate to impose—"

"Impose, nothing," Wynette insisted. "This little darlin' is a joy, and no trouble at all. Now, scoot. Go home, and relax. We'll bring her back safe and sound right after breakfast tomorrow morning."

Shannon hesitated, but the offer was too good to pass up. She couldn't remember when she'd had time to herself, just for herself. "On one condition," she said to Donna Jean.

"Name it."

"That you let me keep Josh one night so you and Neal, *and* you and Ellis can have an evening out."

"You got a deal."

After strict instructions to Lily on minding her manners, Shannon kissed her daughter, said her goodbyes, and headed home in the old truck Ellis had loaned them.

On the short drive home, Wynette's words, *an honest man*, kept playing in her head like an old phonograph album with the needle stuck. The first night she had come into his house she had agreed there would be no more lies between them.

But she hadn't known what a loving, generous man he was then. She hadn't known what life with Jared could be like. Not that her lack of knowing excused the fact that she had lied. It didn't.

But she hadn't loved him then. And she did now.

Wynette had come close to being physic today, Shannon thought. She *had* gazed down at little Josh, and thought about holding Jared's baby. The realization of how much she longed to hold his child in her arms was like a fist to her gut.

She loved Jared. Loved him so much it hurt.

She wanted their life together to be real. She was living her dream, and she didn't want to give it up. But would her dream turn into a nightmare when Jared found out that she had come to him under false pretenses? Of course there were no more pretenses, and what she felt for Jared was definitely not false. But would that make a difference to him?

Thanksgiving was only two days away, and never in Shannon's life—with the possible exception of the day Lily was born—did she have so much to be thankful for. And so much to lose.

THE POP AND CRACKLE that proceeded a transmission woke her up. "Shannon."

She picked up the handheld radio and depressed the talk button. "Jared? Where are you?" The digital clock read 4:14 in the morning.

"Go to channel two."

She did, but suddenly her stomach knotted with anxiety. Channel two was their private channel. "Are you all right?"

"I'm fine."

"You're not bleeding anywhere, are you?"

He laughed. "Over a couple of guys trying for a trophy kill? Not a chance."

"That's a relief," she sighed.

"You shouldn't worry so much."

"Too bad, Game Warden Markham. I worry every time you leave the house."

"Must mean you care."

Shannon yawned. "Or I'm crazy."

There was a long stretch of dead air before he asked, "If you had to pick one right now, which would it be?"

She went very still. "I care," she said softly.

She wasn't sure but she thought she heard him sigh in relief. "I'll be home in ten minutes," was all he said.

"I'll be waiting," she promised, knowing she was promising much more.

Shannon threw back the covers, and slipped out of bed. Going to the closet, she pulled out a pair of jeans and a blouse, then stopped. If she greeted him fully dressed he might get the message that although she cared, she wasn't ready to take their relationship to the next level. Namely, intimacy. But greeting him in her gown and robe could be sending a too blatant message. . . .

"Oh, to hell with it," Shannon whispered to the darkness as she put on her robe, and tied the sash around her waist. She had just told the man she cared about him. Neither one of them was foolish enough to think that meant she wanted to go steady.

She dashed to the bathroom. As she frantically ran a brush through her hair in hopes of looking even moderately appealing, she heard him brake the truck to a stop in the driveway. As usual, his speed amazed her. By the time she closed the bedroom door, and raced to the landing, his hand was on the newel post, one foot on the bottom stair. She flew down the steps, hesitated for a second when she got to the bottom, then went straight into his arms.

His uniform was cool and damp from his time in the hills, but she didn't care. This was what she wanted. This was the only reality that mattered.

"Shannon, Shannon," he murmured against her mouth.

He had kissed her before, but this was different. This time there was no teasing, no restraints. He was kissing her for real. Her head spun, her knees went weak, and she could have sworn she heard her own blood racing, heating in her veins. Never in her life had she felt so sane and delirious, so powerful and fragile, all at the same time. His mouth, warm and demanding, drank from hers. His hands, strong and confident, moved over her. And she simply let the sensation take her wherever he led.

She had kissed him back before, but this, too, was different. This time she held nothing back. This was a fire-meets-fire kiss. An unmistakable, you-want-what-I-want kiss. Jared had to caution himself not to devour her mouth. Not to devour her. Oh, but he wanted to. She was so hot, and he was so needy.

He could have gone on tasting her mouth forever. Silky, smooth and warm. He took the kiss deeper, and was rewarded with a throaty moan, the soft sounds almost shoving him over the edge of control. With his mouth still on hers, he pulled her with him into the living room only a few feet from the stairs until they were in front of the sofa. Then he proceeded to seduce her mouth, slowly, deliberately, as his hands freed the sash of her robe. He opened the garment, and pushed it off her shoulders. If he had expected the gown beneath to be plain cotton, he was in for a shock. It was red, silk and short. Middle-of-her-thighs short. And it clung to her breasts and narrow hips like a lover's caress. Jared's hand trembled as he reached out and gently stroked her small, firm breast through the thin silk.

She quivered, her breath catching in her throat as he continued to stroke her, pet her, until her nipples were hard. When he cupped her fully, she sighed his name.

"You're beautiful," he whispered, kissing her mouth, her throat, the enticing curve of her breasts.

Any concerns of modesty quickly vanished under the heat of his gaze. "I—I— You make me feel beautiful."

With a moan of pleasure, she wrapped her arms around his neck, and her body melted into his. She wanted to be close to him, so close her skin felt like his, and vice versa. When he lifted her off her feet then lay her on the sofa she reached for him, her eyes intense with desire. "Jared, please . . ."

Seeing her lying there, hearing her call for him was ecstasy . . . and agony.

She was his. His alone.

But he couldn't take her. Whatever part of his brain that still produced rational thought told him to get himself under control. Told him this was Shannon, a woman to be treasured, respected. Loved. And as much as he wanted her, he reminded himself that they were not alone. What if Lily woke up, and came looking for her mother?

"I—we can't do this."

Shannon couldn't believe what he was saying. Could there be any question in his mind that she was willing? Surely not. "Jared, I want you. Can't you see how much I want you?"

"Yes," he whispered, a bit dazed that he had called a halt to something they both wanted so badly. But he had to.

Beginning to feel embarrassed, she sat up, reaching for her robe. "I thought . . ." She gazed up at him, confused, hurt. "Don't you . . . don't you want me?"

Jared scrubbed his hands over his face. "So bad it hurts."

"Then I don't understand. Did I do something wrong?" She had only been with one man, and it suddenly crossed her mind that perhaps her experience was too limited for him. "Something you didn't like?"

"No. You were—are—perfect. Shannon . . ."

"Jared you're scaring me. Tell me, please. What's wrong?"

He all but collapsed beside her on the sofa. "Lily."

"What about Lily?"

"I couldn't bear to hurt her."

"Of course not. What does it have to do with—"

"What if she came looking for you, and found us . . . you know? She might be frightened or angry or—"

"She won't come looking for me."

"How can you be so sure? If she wakes and you're not in bed with her—"

"She's not here."

"What?"

"She's spending the night at Wynette and Ellis's house."

"The night? You mean . . . that means we're—"

"Alone."

He gazed into her eyes for several seconds, then stood up and held out his hand. Without a word, she took it and they went upstairs. At the landing, he hesitated. At first Shannon didn't understand why, then she realized he was once again putting control in her hands. He was giving her the opportunity to choose. His bedroom, or hers. Try as she might, Shannon didn't feel right making love to him in the bed that he had shared with another woman.

"Come with me." She pulled him toward her room.

When he closed the door behind them, it took every ounce of self-control he held not to toss her on the bed and devour her. Gently, he reminded himself, without much success. Amy had always needed tenderness, and out of love for his wife he had learned to temper the beast in himself. Now, the wildness in him clawed its way toward freedom, and the tether on his control was weak at best.

"Shannon—"

"Just kiss me."

His mouth was fire on hers, burning, blazing. She welcomed the heat, courted it, even as she felt him try to control the flame. His lack of control didn't scare her. This was Jared. He was not to be compared to anyone before. She trusted him with her life. And her heart. She didn't need gentleness, and she tried to tell him so, but her lips were too busy for speaking. Instead, she let her body tell him. She wrapped her arms around him, her own greed more than evident in the way she met him hunger for hunger.

"I need you," she whispered.

His own need was beyond verbalization as he pulled her into his arms, kissing her harder, deeper. Her mouth was so hot and wet, he thought he might just die from the pure pleasure of her taste. He feasted on her mouth, and still wasn't satisfied. It was as if he had waited all his life to kiss this woman, just this way. If he had expected her to be willing and pliant, he was in for a shock, or a treat, depending on the point of view. What he got was willing, no doubt about it. But he also got wild. And hungry. And hot.

He slipped the straps of her nightgown off her shoulders leaving her bare to the waist. He crushed her to him, running his hands over her back, down to her hips, then under her gown. She wore nothing beneath the silk. No panties. Just Shannon. Soft, smooth, wonderful Shannon. He thought his body might snap in two from the tension, but he couldn't bring himself to stop touching her.

"Take it off," she demanded, but when he reached for her gown she was way ahead of him. In one swift movement a slash of red silk flew across the room. It landed on the rocking chair. "No, I mean you."

Her words snapped the lease on the beast. "Sweet heaven. You're driving me crazy."

"Yeah?" Frantically, she worked at the buttons on his shirt. "Just as long as we go together."

"That's a given." He reached down to unbuckle his holster, and discovered his fingers were almost useless, until . . .

She yanked the shirt free of his pants, shoved it away and put her mouth—her wicked, wicked mouth—on his bare skin.

"Hurry."

"Sh-Shannon," he whispered, rocked to the core. His fingers went from fumbling to frenzied, and in seconds he was as naked as she was.

They tumbled onto the bed. Jared had just enough restraint left to taste her, to worship the satin softness of her breasts, her belly. But she wouldn't let him linger, as she writhed under his touch. Maddened by her response, he brought his mouth to hers again, crushing her lips as he filled her.

Gasping with pleasure, she arched her back, forcing him deeper, straining for more as her body tightened, climbing that ever-spiraling staircase to release.

And Jared was with her heat for heat, stroke for stroke. Together they flew over the moon. She cried out his name, sounding very close to a sob. Her name exploded from his lips on an oath, or a benediction. It didn't matter. The only thing that was important was that their souls joined.

THE SUN WAS SHINING when Shannon opened her eyes. She smiled, gazing at the landscape of Jared's broad and deliciously naked back. So delicious, in fact, that she couldn't resist a taste. She raised up on her elbow, and kissed him ever so lightly on the shoulder.

"Hmm," he murmured into his pillow. "That feels good."

"Tastes better."

He rolled over to face her. "Careful." He lifted a wave of dark hair from her bare shoulder, his fingers skimming her neck. "I might bite back."

"I'll risk it, if you will." Her eyes darkened, sparked with desire.

Jared pulled her into his arms. "Good morning."

"Morning."

"For a minute I thought I was still dreaming."

"Still?"

"Last night must have been a dream because it was like nothing I've ever experienced in real life. It was..."

"Wild?" She had done and felt things with him she hadn't even known she was capable of. It scared her. And excited her. Maybe she had been too wild.

"Incredible. You were incredible. We were incredible together."

"I thought so."

"We were. It's never been like that. So free, so . . ."

"Wild."

He grinned. "Oh, yeah."

"You liked it."

"Let me think." He rubbed his hand over his jaw, seemingly lost in concentration. "You know, for the sake of being fair and honest, maybe we should try it again. Just so I can be sure."

"A comparison test?"

"Something like that." Shannon gasped as he lifted her on top of him. "Something like this."

"Oh, oh-h. Jared? Jared!" She gasped again as he slid into her.

With his hands on her fanny he moved slowly, deliberately. "You may not have much to say, but I like the way you say it."

"But we can't—oh, oh, oh-h-h-h. I..." Her bones were melting. She was sure of it. "I guess we can." And they did.

AFTERWARD, THEIR arms and legs entwined, their sweat-slick bodies recovering from the passion, Jared stroked her hair.

Free. Never in his life had he felt so free or peaceful. Shannon had liberated him from a prison he hadn't even known he was holding himself in until she came along. She was his springtime, sweet, fresh and exhilarating, and he loved her totally, completely.

But how did she feel about him?

Oh, he knew she cared about him. Last night was proof positive that she cared deeply, but that wasn't the same thing as love. Not the kind of love he wanted from her. The kind of love that would last them a lifetime. That's what he wanted. To be with her until they were both old and gray, to love her, to help her raise Lily. And, he realized, he had wanted that practically from the first day she arrived. From where he stood, the future was as sure and true as his love for Shannon.

But where did Shannon stand? What would her answer be if he asked her to marry him?

While a part of him wanted to get down on bended knee and propose, another part cautioned that he might be pressuring her for a decision she wasn't ready to make. And he didn't want to rush her. But he didn't want to lose her. He couldn't lose her. Instinctively, Jared pulled her closer.

Shannon snuggled into his embrace, reveling in the absolute joy of loving Jared. Their night together had been perfect. No, beyond perfect. For the first time in her life she realized how it could be, should be, between a man and a woman. For the first time she understood the difference between sex and making love. As clichéd as it sounded, the difference was that simple, overused, media-exploited, four-letter word. *Love.*

While an inner voice warned her that Jared was not the kind of man to play house for long without wanting to take the next logical step in their relationship, Shannon simply wanted to enjoy the moment without thinking too far ahead. She just wanted to stay here in his arms and leave the rest of the world outside.

At that moment Jared's stomach growled. "I think my stomach is reminding me that I was in such a hurry to get home to you last night that I forgot to eat dinner."

"You know," Shannon said, yawning, "I don't think we even locked the back door last night."

"Don't worry. I know the law in these parts. Besides, I have reliable neighbors."

"Neighbors! Oh, my stars." She sat up in bed. "Jared, Wynette and Ellis are bringing Lily home this morning right after breakfast."

"What time is it?"

The sound of two hoots from the horn of Ellis's pickup truck made a clock unnecessary.

They scrambled out of bed, Jared looking for his clothes, Shannon grabbing a sheet.

"I'll go down and stall them while you get dressed," she said, trying to run to her closet and hold the sheet around her. She reached inside, snatched a pair of jeans and stepped into them.

"Okay."

She yanked open a drawer, pulled out a bra, then T-shirt. Faster, and with more expertise than any man had accomplished in the reverse, she had both on and was stuffing the T-shirt into her jeans, at the same time looking for her shoes. "I'll tell them I let you sleep late."

"Fine, but—"

She shooed him out of the room. "Just hurry up before they start asking questions I can't answer fast enough."

After Wynette's comments the afternoon before, Shannon decided it wouldn't take much for her friend to put two and two together, and come up with an "I told you so." As soon as Jared was on his way back to his room, she washed her face, ran a brush through her hair, and raced down the stairs. The threesome was stepping onto the back porch just as she entered the kitchen.

"Hi." She smiled. And prayed she could—they could—pull this off. "Did you have a good time, Lily?"

Thirty minutes later as they watched Ellis's truck jolting down the driveway, Shannon turned to Jared. "You think they suspect anything?"

"Like the fact that we were making mad passionate love about two minutes before they arrived? Or maybe that you looked like you had just tumbled out of bed—"

"I had."

"—and I looked like a cat who'd just devoured a bowl of cream. Naw." He put his arm around her. "They didn't suspect a thing."

Shannon had a good idea that at least part of her Thanksgiving holiday would include the third degree from Wynette. But that was tomorrow, she thought. And for now, she wanted to savor every moment with Jared. Just once, she wanted to pretend that there was going to be a happily ever after.

8

ALL THROUGH THE DAY, Shannon pretended. It was easy to do—she was gloriously happy.

Because of the long and late hours Jared had been putting in, plus the fact that he had worked on most of the holidays for the last two years, he had today *and* Thanksgiving Day off. He decided an all day trip into Alpine for some shopping was in order, along with a visit to the Woodward Agate Ranch. So, after a quick breakfast, they all piled into Jared's truck, and headed for Alpine.

The first stop was at the feed store, to buy fertilizer for a garden Jared planned to start. Then, they stopped at a toy store to buy Lily a doll which Shannon insisted Lily didn't need, but he purchased anyway. The third stop was for lunch. As they walked through the door of the café, Wynette greeted them with a big smile.

"Well now, don't y'all look like a happy bunch."

"I get to hunt—" Lily turned her smiling face up to Jared. "What's that thing?"

"Agates."

"Uh-huh. Ag-its and Optals. Jared said a princess has to have jewels." She beamed proudly. "And I'm a princess."

"That you are, sweet pea." Wynette grinned at Lily, then said to Jared, "Must be goin' over to Woodward's."

He nodded and looked down at Lily. "So, princess," he said as he fished a quarter out of his pocket, "how about helping me play some music?"

"Yes, yes." She jumped up and down.

"Looks like Jared has fallen head over heels in love," Wynette said, leading Shannon to a booth while Lily led Jared off by the hand.

Shannon's head snapped around. "What?"

"With your daughter."

"Oh . . . yes." She slid into a booth not far from the jukebox. "Believe me, the feeling is mutual."

"Yeah. I could tell that this morning."

Shannon didn't dare make eye contact with Wynette unless she was prepared to deal with a barrage of questions. Some of which she didn't have the answers for.

"So . . . what time do you think y'all will be over tomorrow?"

"T-tomorrow," she stuttered, grateful Wynette had decided not to question her. "Uh, didn't you say the turkey would be done around eleven?"

Wynette plopped two menus onto the table. "Close enough. Bet you never thought you'd be eating a holiday dinner with Jared that first day you walked in here."

"No, I sure didn't."

"I can tell you now that even though I prodded him into that ad, I wasn't holdin' my breath. I figured if he even got a date out of it, he'd be lucky. And look what he got."

"I don't know how lucky he is—"

"Hey, you're the best thing that's happened to that big yahoo in a long time. Take my word for it. Why, just a few days ago I was braggin' about the two of you."

"Bragging?"

"There was a couple of hunters in here, and I was tellin' them about how romantic it was, you and Jared findin' each other kinda sight unseen as it were."

"Hunters?" Alarm bells went off in Shannon's head.

"Well, sorta. You know, all dressed up in army clothes."

Shannon's mouth went dry. "From around here?"

"Naw. There's usually a dozen or so come out here once or twice a year to play those phony war games. Lord knows we got enough space."

Survivalists. Hal's kind of people. With her heart pounding in her ears, Shannon had to struggle to keep her voice from betraying the sheer terror that had gripped her like talons. "These, uh, hunters you were talking to. I'll bet they thought the story was mushy."

"Nope. They were real interested. We weren't very busy that day, and you know me, I love to visit. But it was kinda nice to see that a couple of real macho guys could appreciate a happy ending."

"Happy ending?"

"You, Lily and Jared. A nice little family." She winked at Shannon. "And don't tell me I'm imagin' things. I saw how you two were tryin' not to look at each other this morning."

Thankfully she didn't have to comment on Wynette's observation because at that moment, Jared and Lily approached the booth. "We're starved," Jared announced.

"Can I have a cheese sandwich, please, Wynette?" Lily asked, crawling in beside her mother.

"You sure can, sweet pea. With extra pickles and chips."

"I'll take a burger, double meat, French fries and a vanilla malt." Jared looked over at Shannon, a decidedly wicked gleam in his eyes. "I've developed a taste for vanilla ice cream lately."

Shannon smiled, praying her eyes didn't betray the panic screaming through her mind. The last time Hal found them was with the help of a fellow gun collector that had seen them, and called the gun club he belonged to. Hal had also circulated a flyer, with a picture of her and Lily on it, amongst his gun-toting, Saturday morning soldier friends. What if these men related Wynette's story to some of their comrades in arms, then those men told it to others, and so on? Was it possible Hal could pick up such a slight lead, and track them down?

Anything was possible, she reminded herself. And she had learned the hard way not to underestimate her

ex-husband's blind determination. It would be bad
enough if he found them, but if he found her with another man... She didn't even want to think about what
he might do to Jared.

"Shannon?"

"What?"

"I asked if you were ready to order."

"Oh, uh...I'm not as hungry as I thought I was. You
and Lily go ahead."

"Are you sure?"

She nodded. "I'll get something later."

Until this moment she hadn't fully considered what
might happen to Jared if he and Hal should ever cross
paths. Jared was sworn to uphold the law, and techni-
cally *she* was a lawbreaker. Even though she had cus-
tody of Lily, the court had granted Hal visitation rights.
Not that he had ever used them, but she had taken his
daughter out of the state without permission. Dear
Lord, what if Hal showed up with some kind of court
order, and Jared was forced to turn her over to the authorities?

Or worse. What if Hal decided to include Jared in his
thirst for revenge? If anything happened to Jared because of her, she wouldn't be able to live with herself.

Shannon made it through lunch without looking
over her shoulder every time someone came into the
café, and finally her panic receded. But it wasn't until
they were out of Alpine headed for their rock hunt that
she began to feel more at ease. She told herself she was

overreacting. Hal couldn't possibly know where they were. Almost four weeks had gone by without so much as a glimpse of him. But how many times had she been into town in that time? Twice. Three times, at the most. He could easily have missed seeing her—

Stop it. Stop it right now, she warned herself, knowing the more she worried, the bigger the worry became. No, Hal was in West Virginia. She and Lily were safe. And she was making a mountain out of a molehill. Besides, Jared knew how to handle men like Hal.

But then that was part of the problem now, wasn't it? Unintentionally, she had involved the one person other than Lily whom she wanted to protect.

For the rest of the day Shannon forced herself not to think about the hunters. Instead, every time a worrisome thought popped into her head, she glanced at Jared. One look at this man who had made her happier in a few short weeks than she could ever remember, and the dark thoughts were pushed aside.

They drove to the Woodward Ranch, and were able to join a group of tourists ready to hunt. Shannon focused her attention on the guide as he explained that the ranch was known for the red plume agate, called dendritic agate, which was formed in gas pockets of lava. He told them that the beauty came from iron crystals trapped in the rock, and that Woodward agate was so well-known because it formed a feather or tree design.

The day was sunny with a light breeze, and the outing proved to be not only great fun, put productive. To

Lily's delight, she found two quality agates, quickly labeled "her treasure." And to Shannon's joy and amazement, she too, found several exceptional stones. But nothing compared to the small opals that Jared discovered.

"Thank you for a wonderful day," Shannon told him later that evening as they sat in the front porch swing. Lily had just gone to bed. Dusk was creeping up on the night, and the stars were warming up to twinkle.

"My pleasure. I think we may have quite a little rock hound on our hands. Lily was a natural."

"She was, wasn't she? But you were the big winner. Those opals were small, but so lovely."

He smiled. "They don't even compare to your eyes, or your skin." He nuzzled her neck.

"Hmm, flattery. Continue."

"Let's see, now. How about, incredibly sexy?"

"Sexy is good."

He lifted her dark hair from her neck and kissed her earlobes. "You can say that again."

Shannon sighed, fully relaxing for the first time today. "Sexy is good."

"Think you're cute, don't you?"

"Don't you? I think you're awfully cute."

"Men aren't cute. They're handsome or distinguished or—"

"Sexy?"

"I'll take what I can get." He pulled her to him and kissed her long and hard. "Shannon," he said against her temple.

"Hmm."

"I—I need to tell you something."

She could feel his body tense. "It must be serious."

"Yeah, serious. But I need to say it, so bear with me."

"All right."

"That first day, when you and Lily came home with me, I had some preconceived notions about how things would be if you stayed. I thought all I wanted, all I needed was for us to be friends. Figured that was the best I could hope for. But I was wrong. I don't want to be your friend. I want to be your best friend. But I also want to be the one who makes your eyes sparkle with desire. I want to be the one who touches you, holds you. I love you, Shannon. I think I've loved you since the minute I walked in, and found you waiting up for me that first time."

Stunned and thrilled, she couldn't form a thought, much less a coherent sentence.

When she didn't answer, Jared's courage deflated like a punctured balloon. His heart felt as if it had suddenly been ripped in two. With a groan, he sat forward on the swing and put his head in his hands. "You weren't expecting this. I rushed you. I'm sorry. Things happened so quickly. Last night . . . I wanted you. It was wonderful. Beyond anything I had ever dreamed. But . . . Oh, hell, I'm babbling like an idiot. What I'm trying to say—" He looked up, and saw the tears on her lashes, and his heart sank. "You're crying. Oh, God, I've made a mess of this."

"Jared."

"Now you're hurt, and crying—"

"Jared."

"I never meant to hurt you—"

"Jared." She took his face in her hands. The action accomplished what her words couldn't. He stopped talking. "I'm not crying because you hurt me."

"You're not?"

What lucky star had she been born under to finally stumble across this marvelous man? she wondered. Maybe he was her reward for what she had been through. Maybe it was just fate. What difference did it make? He loved her. He loved her!

"I'm crying because you love me, and it's so wonderful."

"It is?" His hands covered hers, then he pulled them to his lips. "It is. And before you say anything else, I want you to know I don't expect you to say you love me back. I know—at least I think I know—that you have feelings for me, but they may not be love. And that's okay. But I love you and Lily, and I want you both in my life."

This all sounded suspiciously like a proposal.

She should have known after last night. Jared wasn't the kind of man who took making love to a woman lightly. She should have seen this coming. What a fool she had been. She had created this nice little fantasy for herself, and now reality was knocking at the door. He would be hurt when he learned she had lied to him. He would be hurt, and ashamed to learn he had asked a liar to marry him. Near panic, she had to stop him before he made, and asked for a commitment she couldn't give, no matter how desperately she wanted to. "Shannon—"

"We're in your life."

"Yes, and—"

"Can't we let that be enough for now?"

"No." He put a hand under her chin and tilted her head so that he could look into her eyes. "We can't. I want more."

"Jared—"

"Much more."

Please don't, she prayed. Don't ask. "Jared, don't—"

"I want to marry you. Live with you, love you forever. I want to be a father to Lily, and someday watch you hold our child in your arms."

Oh, he was killing her. "Aren't we...rushing things?"

"Are we? You've known from the moment you read my ad in that damned magazine that marriage was my ultimate goal. This isn't a news flash."

He was angry, and he had every right to be. "Of course not, but I thought we agreed—"

"You and I made love last night, or did I dream that?"

"No, but—"

"Then help me understand what's going on here. What had you planned on doing if our arrangement worked out to your satisfaction? Live in sin?"

"No, of course not."

"Then what?"

"I don't know. I . . . I wasn't expecting this. You said it yourself. Everything has happened so quickly."

"But last night—"

"Was the most beautiful night of my life. You're a wonderful lover. A wonderful man. Any woman would be lucky to have you. I—I just want to be sure. Can you understand that?"

She knew it was a lame excuse. It was as weak as she had been.

"All I understand is that if you're not sure after what happened between us last night, then maybe you're not the woman I thought you were."

Without a backward glance, he went inside, leaving her alone.

THANKSGIVING MORNING dawned cool and crisp. Inside the Markham homestead as well as outside. Breakfast was a rather somber affair with poor Lily totally confused about why her two favorite people in the world didn't look happy. By the time they all got dressed, packed up the food they were taking, loaded everything, including the dogs into the truck, then drove to the Dickerson ranch, the tension was as thick as cold gravy. Shannon was relieved when Jared disappeared into the den to join the other men in front of the television. Lily too, made herself scarce, going outside to play with Mack and Pit.

"What put a burr under his saddle?" Wynette asked immediately.

"Me, I'm afraid."

"Wanna talk about it?"

Shannon shook her head.

"Let me know if you change your mind."

The Thanksgiving meal with all the traditional trimmings, plus a few Texas additions such as salsa and tortillas, was served shortly after noon. When everyone was finally seated around the long dining table, Ellis asked that everybody hold hands while he said grace. Jared was sitting next to her, and for a moment Shannon thought he might refuse to take her hand. But he entwined his fingers with hers, and for a split second after the amen she thought he squeezed her hand. After everyone was stuffed and relaxed, the men once again drifted back to the football games, and the women began cleaning up.

The children of one of the ranch hands came to the back door, asking if Lily could play, and Shannon gave her permission. Why shouldn't at least one of them have a nice day? she thought.

Shannon, Wynette and Donna Jean had just finished washing the dishes, and had started on the pots and pans when they heard Lily scream. Shannon dropped the skillet she had been drying, and headed for

the door, but before she could open it, one of the other
children came bursting into the kitchen.

"Ms. Dickerson, come quick! The fire ants got Lily!"

Shannon nearly knocked the child down in her haste
to get through the door. Behind her she heard Jared's
heavy step.

Jared got to Lily before she did. Frantically, he swatted at Lily's legs, with almost no effect. To Shannon's
horror her daughter's legs were literally covered in ants
almost up to her knees. Parts of her hands, arms and
neck were also dotted with ants. Screaming hysteri-
cally, Lily swatted at herself, and tried to reach out for
Shannon at the same time.

"Oh, baby—"

"Don't touch her. They'll be all over you," Jared
yelled, his own hands already dotted with ants.

"My God, Jared—"

"They're inside her clothes. Get 'em off," someone
hollered out.

But Jared was way ahead of them. He yanked Lily up
into his arms, and raced to the side of the house where
a garden hose was connected to a faucet. In five seconds he had Lily stripped to her bare feet and panties,
and was hosing the vicious insects off her trembling
body.

Practically hysterical herself, Shannon stood two feet
away, sobbing, waiting to snatch her traumatized child
into her arms.

"Neal, get a towel outta the bathroom right quick to dry her off," Wynette ordered. "Poor little thing. She musta been standing in an ant bed to get so many on her so quick."

"We were playin' hide and seek," one of the kids said. "She was countin' with her eyes closed."

"Here you go." Neal came running out of the house with a towel, and handed it to Shannon just about the time Jared was satisfied Lily had been washed clean.

Choking back a sob, Shannon flung the towel around Lily, and hugged her to her. "Shh, shh, baby. It's okay." Lily's little body shook violently. "Everything is going to be all right." Shannon was none too steady herself.

"Gimme that hose." Ellis said, taking it from Jared. "You got'em all over you." He proceeded to hose off Jared's hands and arms, soaking his shirt and jeans in the process.

"Wynette, I need a blanket to wrap her in so she doesn't get chilled before we get to the hospital," Jared stated.

Shannon's head snapped up. "Hospital?" Insect bites weren't trivial, but Lily had no insect allergies. She didn't understand why Jared thought a hospital was necessary.

"Ellis, will you call ahead and let them know we're coming?"

But Neal was already headed toward the house. "I'm on it."

"Jared—"

"No, Neal. Let Ellis do that." He pitched his set of keys to Neal. "Equipment box in the bed of my truck. First aid kit. Will you put it up front?"

"Done," Neal said as he dashed off.

"Jared?" Shannon swallowed another rising tide of panic.

"We don't have much time," he told her calmly. "Fire ant bites are like bee stings. Highly toxic. Lily needs to see a doctor. Now."

Holding her sobbing child close, her brain on overload, she still didn't understand what he was trying to tell her. Then Jared reached down, and flipped back one corner of the towel. Shannon's eyes widened in shock.

Both Lily's legs were red, and already swollen.

"Oh, my God," Shannon whispered, her terrified gaze meeting Jared's even as he was reaching for Lily.

Everybody moved at once, and miraculously, by the time they reached the truck the blanket was there, the first aid kit was on the front seat, and the motor was running. Jared helped Shannon in, set Lily in her lap, threw the blanket over them, jumped behind the wheel, and they were off in a spray of gravel.

Shannon had no idea how much time had actually passed, but it felt like hours. Long, terrifying hours. In her arms, Lily whimpered, her body feverish. And just when they drove into Alpine and Shannon thought everything would be okay, Lily's breathing became labored. She was almost gasping for air.

"Do you know CPR?" Jared asked.

Shannon's heart leapt into her throat. Wide-eyed, she shook her head. Jared's grim expression and white-knuckled grip on the steering wheel testified to the fact that the situation was getting worse, not better. Minutes later he whipped the truck into the parking lot of the Alpine hospital, killed the engine, ran to the passenger side, and practically yanked the door off its hinges. A second later Shannon found herself in the middle of the tiny emergency room in another frenzy of people.

And Jared was like the center ring of a wheel, holding all the spokes together while the hospital staff did their job. His voice was calm as he related where and when the ant attack had taken place, and as she listened it was easy to believe that nothing bad could happen to her child as long as Jared was there. As long as she had his calm, steady presence beside her.

Lily was immediately put on oxygen, and after establishing that she had no allergies, she was given an injection of antihistamines, and a topical cream to aid in reducing the swelling, and to prevent her from scratching the bites. The emergency-room doctor explained that most children responded to the treatment within a half hour, but to be on the safe side he had also phoned a pediatrician to take a look at Lily. Sure enough, within twenty minutes Shannon began to see a change for the better. Lily's breathing became easier, and she seemed more comfortable. If Jared's strong arm hadn't been around her, Shannon thought she might have collapsed from relief. A short time later a nurse came in and requested forms be filled out and questions answered concerning Lily's general health.

"I don't want to leave her," Shannon said when the nurse insisted.

"Go fill out the forms. I won't leave her side until you get back," Jared promised.

Shannon went, reluctantly. As she was completing the last of the tedious forms the doctor came out.

"Ms. Kramer, I think your little girl is going to be just fine. If you had waited another ten or fifteen minutes, it might have been a different story. Those ant bites are bad enough for adults, but they can be lethal for kids. But she's responding to treatment very well." He pulled a prescription pad from his pocket, and began writing. "This is for more antihistamines. A little stronger than what you can buy over the counter, so you can expect her to sleep a lot. Let her. The more she sleeps, the less she will scratch the bites, and the less chance there is of infection setting in."

"Thank you, doctor. Thank you for everything."

"You're welcome. Now, I'm going to let you take her home in about an hour. If you've got any Epsom salts you might try putting some in her bath water to ease the itching. And I'd like you to call me tomorrow and let me know how she's doing."

"Thank you, again." Shannon couldn't help it, she started crying all over again. "I'm just so grateful—"

"Now don't you worry. A week from now you'll be scolding her for leaving her toys out, and all of this will be just a memory. I saw her give her daddy a great big smile not two minutes ago, so she's on the mend."

"Oh, but he's—" Before she could finish her protest a nurse called the doctor to the phone. He excused himself and took the call. Shannon went in to see Lily.

IT WAS DARK by the time they got home. Again wrapped in the blanket Wynette had loaned them, Jared carried a sleeping Lily upstairs.

Knowing everyone at the Dickersons would be anxious for news, they had called before leaving the hospital to assure them Lily would be fine.

At the top of the stairs, Jared turned to Shannon. "Why don't you go to the kitchen and get a glass of water in case she wakes up and needs more of that stuff the doctor prescribed?" he asked. "I'll put her to bed. You can dress her later."

"All right," she whispered.

Returning with the water, she heard Jared talking. "Oh, princess. You scared me to death today."

Shannon stopped outside the room.

"Do you know how precious you've become to me? I would die rather than let anything happen to you. But today I felt so helpless. Lily, sweet Lily. Thank God, you're all right."

Shannon heard his voice break, and her heart shattered into a million pieces.

It seemed like years ago that she had come up with the perfect way to start a new life for her and her child. She should have known when she saw Jared rescue that young skateboarder that she was doomed to love him. Real-life heroes don't grow on trees, and she had stumbled across one by pure accident.

And she would be a fool to turn her back and walk away from him.

She realized that she had lived with fear for so long that she couldn't see past it to what a normal existence could be. Until now. Here was what she had been looking for all along. He was the man she needed forever. He was the answer to her prayers.

"Jared." She stepped inside the door.

He had been kneeling beside the bed, and stood up when she entered. "That stuff really knocked her out," he said, keeping his voice low.

"I know."

"You think she'll sleep through the night?"

"I think so."

"If she wakes up—" he looked at Shannon "—will you call me?"

"Yes. I promise."

He nodded, and left the room. Shannon took one of Lily's gowns out of the drawer, and put it on her. Lily never stirred, but slept on peacefully.

But Shannon knew peace would elude her until she faced Jared with the truth.

He was on the back porch, the dogs at his feet. The light from the low-wattage yellow bug light cast the area in pale outlines and gray shadows.

"I think Mack and Pit know that she's sick," Jared said when she took the chair across from him. "Animals have a sense about the humans they bond with." As if on cue, Pit went to the door, whined, then came back, lay down and put his head on his paws.

"Jared, I want you to know how grateful—"

"Don't." He held up a hand. "I don't deserve gratitude."

"Of course you do. You saved my daughter's life today."

"No, I didn't."

"Jared, I'm not going to sit here and argue the point. If you hadn't thought of using that garden hose, I shudder to think what might have happened to Lily. So, whether you want to hear it or not, thank you. You're the bravest man I've ever known."

"How can you say that?" The words almost exploded out of him. "You know that I couldn't even save my wife. My own child."

She reached out and held his hand. "Being brave doesn't mean you always succeed. Being brave means you try, and you keep on trying. And letting someone look into your heart in the place you're most afraid of is the purist form of bravery. You did that the night little Joshua was born. And again . . . just a few moments ago when you were talking to Lily."

"She's so . . . If anything had happened . . ."

Shannon went to him, and kneeled beside his chair. "It didn't, thanks to you." She stroked his cheek. "I was a fool to think that I could ever walk away from you. I love you, Jared."

"What did you just—"

"I love you."

"Is this your idea of gratitude? You've already said thanks."

"But I haven't told you the truth. I haven't said what's in my heart. Look at me." When he turned to her, she looked straight into his eyes. "I love you, Jared Markham, with all my heart, all my soul."

He stared at her, letting her words sink in. Then he leaned forward, picked her up and put her on his lap, cradling her, holding her. "Oh, Shannon. I love you so."

"I'm sorry I hurt you last night. I didn't mean to."

"It's forgotten."

"No, Jared. I have to explain why—"

"It doesn't make any difference. Whatever your concerns, we can work them out together. Say it again."

"I love you. I—" The rest was smothered by his kiss.

His lips were warm, tempting and she wanted to give in to the kiss, wanted it to go on forever. But she still had another truth to tell, and she knew if she let herself melt into the kiss, she would never be able to tell him everything.

"Jared, wait. I have to tell you—"

"Doesn't matter." He pulled her to him again.

"Yes it does." She slipped out of his arms, and returned to her own chair. "It matters a great deal. And you have to hear this, or . . . or we . . ." She was painfully aware that there might not be a *we* when she continued, ". . . don't have a chance."

"All right," he said, seeing her determination.

She gathered her courage, held on tight, knowing she would need every ounce. "I . . . I answered your ad under false pretenses. When I came here, I never intended to stay."

"You had reservations. I knew that, but—"

"No, Jared. I lied to you."

9

HE WAS GOING INSANE. That had to be the answer. He'd just been through one of the most horrific days of his life, and she was telling him that she had lied to him? Used him? No, he was experiencing the normal confusion and fatigue after the kind of sustained adrenaline rush that comes with life-and-death situations. He was ready to drop in his tracks. He simply must have heard her wrong.

"I never meant to hurt you. And I would give anything if I didn't have to hurt you now, but I have to tell you the truth."

"The truth?"

"Yes."

"That you used me," he said, his eyes still glazed with confusion.

"To begin with, my ex-husband isn't dead. He's alive. And . . . and I'm what you might call a fugitive. There's probably a warrant out for my arrest in the state of West Virginia."

"You're wanted?"

"Jared, please . . . if you can just listen until I finish, all your questions will be answered. At least I hope they will," she said, wondering if he would ever again ask the one question she wanted to hear. "Promise me, you'll listen before you ask any more questions?"

He nodded.

"My ex-husband, Hal Jackson, didn't want the divorce, but I was determined." She clasped her hands together to keep them from shaking. "Hal was always a physical man. At first it was just an occasional shove then . . ."

She swallowed hard, her eyes stinging with unshed tears. She would not cry! She wanted Jared's understanding, and most of all she wanted his love. She didn't want sympathy.

"You're so secure in your masculinity, but Hal . . . wasn't. He thought we belonged to him, and his ego had been wounded. After the divorce he started harassing me. I did everything by the book. Called the police, got a peace bond, went back to court to get his visitations restricted. I did everything I was supposed to do only . . . Only Hal had *friends*."

The venom in her voice finally cleared the fog from his brain as if a veil had been lifted. She was so rigid she look as if she might snap in two. For the first time since she told him she had lied, the pain in her voice got through to him.

"They were his gun-club friends, and his weekend survival training comrades. All macho maniacs. Lawyers, cops, even a couple of judges. Funny how that worked. I took Hal to court and one of his gun-club buddies turned out to be the judge. Guess who got her hand slapped? Guess who was told she didn't have any choice but to let her unbalanced, raging ex-husband spend time with her four-year-old daughter? When that asinine excuse for a family court judge said, 'A child needs a father,' I wanted to scream. Hal was never a father to Lily."

At this point Shannon got up and gazed out at the peaceful night. "I tried to get away from him. Changed jobs, moved to another town. He always found us. The last time . . ." She shuddered with the memory, then turned to look at Jared. "He said would kill me. Or worse, he would just take Lily and I would never see her again. I believed him. So, we ran, and ran . . ." She took a deep breath, exhaling slowly. "Then one afternoon in a bus station I picked up the magazine and saw your ad. Your home was so remote. I thought that if I could keep Hal off our trail for a few weeks, we could start a new life. It was all so simple. After a time I intended to tell you that I had made a mistake, that it wasn't working for me, then Lily and I would leave. But I hadn't counted on falling in love with you.

"And I know that doesn't mean anything to you now, but it's true. I don't think I knew what real love was until I met you."

For a long time the only sound was the wind whistling through the trees, the occasional distant howl of a coyote or the call of a night bird.

Shannon waited for the questions. And the anger. Lord knew he was entitled.

"The last time?"

"What?"

"What happened the last time he found you?"

The question was so unexpected that for a moment she just stared at him. "I— He tried to strangle me. My landlord showed up or he would have succeeded."

"And Lily?"

Now the tears came. "Sh-she saw it all."

Jared's blistering oath made the dogs jump. "Tell me," he said between clenched teeth. "Tell me he didn't hurt her. If he took out his rage on a helpless child—"

"No. He never touched Lily. In fact, under the circumstances, she's amazingly well-adjusted."

"If the son of a bitch ever crosses my path, that'll probably be the only thing that keeps me from killing him." His gaze met hers. "He's damned close for what he did to you."

Shannon had never seen this side of Jared. This steely-eyed malice toward another human being. Undoubtedly, this was the man poachers and smugglers faced, the man who not only wore a badge but was prepared to back it up. All of that controlled rage, dark and furious, in a man of his size was intimidating. Given her history with Hal, she should have been terrified, but she wasn't. As awesome as she knew his anger to be, it *was* controlled. But there was more to it. Instinctively, maybe even from the first moment they had met, she had trusted him. At least her heart had. It had just taken her head a little longer.

But just because he wasn't aiming his rage at her didn't mean he was willing to forgive her. That was too much to hope for.

"I would give anything if I could go back to that first day, and start over, but I can't."

"You said almost those very words the day we met."

"Did I? That much hasn't changed."

"But we have—I have. I fought loving you, Shannon. You were so different from Amy, and I was convinced I could never love again."

"Jared—"

He held up a hand to silence her. "I can't trivialize lying by saying it doesn't matter, but I understand why you didn't tell me the truth. It's not like you've had a long list of trustworthy people in your life. In a way, it boils down to the self-preservation for you and your child. I can't—won't blame you for that."

"I—I'm not sure I understand what you're saying," she said, daring to hope.

"The first day we met, you told me that you wanted a real home, security. For Lily to be safe and happy. Was that part of the lie?"

"No. Never."

The thrill of her words shot through him, then settled soft and glowing around his heart. "You also told me that you hoped I would find the woman I was looking for."

"I r-remember."

"I found her."

Shannon was afraid to move, to even breathe for fear that this was all a dream. Was he saying what she thought he was saying? Could she be that lucky?

He came to her, lifted a wisp of dark hair then tucked the escapee from her French braid back into place. "We found each other, Shannon. Call it fate, or whatever name you choose. The road we took wasn't exactly conventional, but *we found each other*. The rest of this—" he waved his hand as if in dismissal "—we can deal with. You don't have to run anymore. The question still stands. Will you marry me?"

She was thunderstruck. Marry Jared? Live and love with him for the rest of her life?

Jared tried to read an answer in her eyes, but all he found was a shimmering, stunned expression. He had poured his heart out at her feet, and she would either take it or . . . Without realizing it, he took a step back. If she didn't want him . . .

Shannon did the only thing she could do. She stopped him. Her hand shot out, and grabbed the front of his shirt.

"What are you doing?"

"Giving you my answer," she said, pulling him into her arms, right where he belonged.

"WELL, AT LEAST there's not a warrant out for your arrest."

"Are you sure?" Shannon asked. Jared had been in his office since he finished breakfast making calls on her behalf, and talking to Niles Winston, the lawyer he had asked to handle everything for her. It was now almost noon.

"Winston says you're clean as a whistle."

"I'm surprised."

"Me, too, after what you told me." Jared didn't add that he thought the reason her ex-husband hadn't turned her in was that he wanted to get to her before the law could. Weekend warrior types like Hal Jackson often considered themselves justified in taking the law into their own hands. The thought didn't make him feel any easier, but there was no point in giving Shannon more to worry about.

"Winston is making some inquiries, and trying to keep it discreet, but sooner or later we'll accumulate a paper trail that your ex-husband will be able to track. That means he'll know where you are."

She took a deep breath. "I know."

"And since you did take Lily out of state without the court's permission, eventually you will have to return to West Virginia to clear this mess up once and for all."

"I know that, too." She yanked the sheets from the bed in order to put on fresh linens. "But Jared, what if he shows up here? What if he causes trouble for you?"

"I can take care of myself. As for him showing up here, I have to admit there's a part of me that hopes he does so I can have the pleasure of beating him senseless before I arrest him. He might have some pull in West

Virginia, but if he breaks the law in Texas, his buddies can't do him any good."

"Well, I'm not thrilled about the prospect of going back, but I understand that's what has to happen."

"And you know that this time will be different. They won't take advantage of you like they did before. I'll see to it because I'll be coming with you."

"That's so sweet of you, but—"

"No buts. Do you honestly think I would let you face that creep alone?"

"I can't ask you to drop everything and go with me. The lawyer you hired has already recommended a colleague in West Virginia. It may take days or even weeks. I may have to—"

"We may have to."

"Jared." She straightened from smoothing out the clean sheets. "You can't just take off from your job, and go flying halfway across the country."

"Even game wardens get vacations. I'm going with you, and that's final."

Shannon gave the pillows an extra fluff, and put them on the bed. "At least when I go, I'll be Mrs. Jared Markham."

"I like the sound of that." The sight of her leaning over the bed was just too tempting. He came up behind her, grabbed her by the waist, and spun her around and up against him a split second before they fell onto the bed. "And the feel of you."

"Hey, no fair," she teased, laughing and breathless.

"You know what they say, 'All's fair in love and war.'"
He nuzzled her neck.

This sort of sexual play was new to her, but she was
rapidly getting used to it. It was flirtatious, and fun. She
liked it. Even now, knowing they didn't have the time
to play, she hated to be the one to call it to a halt.

"Uh, need I remind you that Lily is playing in the new
sandbox you made for her right outside the window?"

"She's downstairs, we're up." He nibbled on her ear-
lobe while his hands slid possessively over her hip.

"Sound, ohh, uh . . . travels."

"So be quiet," he whispered against her lips. His
mouth lingered, then gently deepened the kiss.

"Hmm." She barely managed to extricate herself
from the kiss. "As much as I'm enjoying this—" he
reached for her again, but she wiggled away "—we
can't."

Jared rolled onto his back, and threw his arm across
his eyes. "Oh, the rejection."

"I'll show you rejection if you mess up my freshly
made bed."

He lifted his arm, and she caught the wicked little
glint in his eyes. "We could mess it up together."

"No, we couldn't."

When he got off the bed and came toward her, she
started backing up. "Now, Jared, you know what we
decided—"

"Changed my mind."

"It's only one more day. We're getting married to-morrow and—"

He stalked her. "You're too tempting. I'll never make it another hour, much less another day."

She kept backing up. "Oh, yes you can. Jared. Jared, stop right there. Don't you come any—"

At that moment Wynette's rattletrap old station wagon came bouncing into the driveway, horn honking.

Shannon grinned. "Saved by the horn," she said, sidestepping him for a clean getaway.

By the time he came downstairs, Shannon and Wynette were already deep into a discussion about where to place the flowers that had been ordered to decorate the living room where the ceremony was to take place. In planning the wedding, they had gone from just the three of them before a justice of the peace, to a simple home affair with a handful of friends to witness their vows. Only it seemed everyone in Brewster County called Jared a friend.

"With the fireplace, there's really not a lot of wall space," Shannon said.

"Yeah, and you got all those windows on one side and that big old armoire on the other."

"Even with the sofa pushed against the windows, I'm not sure how much room we'll have. What's the count so far?"

"With Tucker and his family, plus a couple of Jared's friends from Marathon, we're up to thirty-five."

Shannon sighed. "Guess everyone will just have to stand."

"Well, if too many show up, we'll just have to stick 'em out on the front porch."

Shannon's eyes lit up. "That's a wonderful idea."

"Leavin' folks on the porch? I was only—"

"What do you think, Jared?"

"Oh, no," he said, in the process of polishing off the sandwich Shannon had made for lunch. "This wedding stuff is strictly off-limits as far as I'm concerned. You ladies do it the way you want. All I have to do is show up with a best man and a ring."

"No, really. What do you think about having the ceremony outside?"

"On the porch?"

"No, silly. In the backyard by the big redbud trees."

"You know," Wynette propped a hand on her hip. "For an idea, that ain't half-bad."

Jared looked down into Shannon's face, flushed with happiness and excitement. She had never looked more beautiful.

"If that's want you want, then go for it."

She squealed, and threw her arms around his neck, pecking kisses all over his face. His arms closed around her. "I'll give you fifteen minutes to stop that."

"Oh, Jared, it'll be wonderful."

With her still in his arms, he dipped his head and kissed her. "You're wonderful. I don't care if we say our

'I do's' in the middle of town, just so long as you're mine by sunset tomorrow."

"Hmm," she said against his mouth.

Wynette cleared her throat. "I hate to break this up, but if you two are gettin' hitched outdoors, we've got some changin' and rearrangin' to do."

"Killjoy," Jared said without malice. "All right." His hands on her waist, he set Shannon away from him. "I can see from this point on, I'll just be in the way. Besides, I've got to be in court in Fort Stockton to testify in a smuggling case at two o'clock." He gave her a quick kiss, and headed out the door.

"Be careful," she called after him.

"We got things to do, and places to go," Wynette announced.

"Where?"

"Alpine. We gotta talk to the florist, go by the hardware store—"

"The hardware store?"

"Sugar, you can't serve food outdoors without some of those bucket candle things to keep the bugs away."

Shannon laughed at her practical, wonderful friend. "Then we'd better get a move on."

"I'll go get Lily cleaned up while you change clothes," Wynette said.

As she climbed the stairs Shannon heard Wynette bribing Lily with the promise of an ice cream cone if she would hurry, and thought that her life just couldn't get any better.

Two hours later, their errands completed, it was time for Wynette to pay up.

"A promise is a promise, and I'm a woman of my word," she told Lily as the three of them exited the hardware store.

"Can I have two dips?" The child looked at her mother, her big eyes soft and pleading.

"You little hustler. Okay. I'm in a generous mood."

"Yippee!" Lily jumped up and down.

They set off toward the ice cream parlor. As they passed a fabric store, Shannon suddenly stopped. "Oh, I need to pick up some ribbon to match the dress Lily is wearing tomorrow."

"Why don't you go ahead? Lily and I will walk on up to the ice cream parlor, and you can catch us after you get your ribbon."

"All right. Save some rocky road for me." Wynette and Lily went ahead, and Shannon went inside. After making her purchase, she set off toward the ice cream store. She stopped at a crosswalk to wait for the light to turn green, and casually glanced across the street.

And her heart almost stopped beating.

There was a man standing outside one of the stores, and he looked exactly like . . .

She blinked, looked again, but the light had changed, and cars were zipping through the intersection, obscuring her view. When she could see the spot clearly again, the man was gone.

It couldn't have been Hal. It couldn't have been.

But her pounding heart wasn't listening. What if he had found them? What if he knew where they lived?

"No," Shannon said out loud, and a passerby gave her a strange look. She was letting her imagination run away with her, that's all. So there was a man with dark curly hair on a street in Alpine, Texas. There were probably hundreds of people matching that description in this town. No reason to go ballistic. She had to get a grip on herself before she joined Wynette and Lily.

Stay calm, she told herself. But she was only moderately successful. In fact, her apprehensiveness increased as she walked on. Once, just before she reached the ice cream store the hair on the back of her neck stood up on edge, and she had the feeling she was being watched. But when she looked around, she saw no one she recognized. Nothing out of the ordinary.

She reminded herself that Hal wasn't a subtle person. He favored the direct bulldozer approach, rather than relying on stealth. In the past when he had discovered their whereabouts, he had simply waited where they lived, and snagged them when they came home. Not once had he ever shown up during the daytime. Shannon breathed a sigh of relief. See there, it couldn't have been Hal. She had just caught sight of a man who looked like him, and panicked for a second. It was just too many months of running. Yes, that was it. A normal response after living in fear for so long. Shannon managed to settle her jangled nerves, and put on a smile as she joined Lily and Wynette, but the incident had left her shaken. And uneasy.

So uneasy, in fact, that even locked safely inside the house, with Jared sleeping only two rooms away, she found herself listening to the night sounds, trying to decipher them. Was that rustling a man sneaking around the yard, or an armadillo rooting for food? Was that twig snapped by a four-legged varmint or a two-legged one?

She was losing it. Tomorrow she was marrying the most loving, sexy man on the planet—in the galaxy—and here she was lying in bed conjuring up bogeymen. All because she looked up and saw a man that she *thought* looked like her ex-husband. What was wrong with her? She didn't have anything to be afraid of anymore. Not while she had Jared.

Oh, maybe this was all just prewedding jitters. After all, it wasn't every day a girl wound up with her heart's desire, and a prince charming to boot.

Shannon closed her eyes, and took a deep breath. Tomorrow was the beginning of more happiness than any woman had a right to dream of. She would not think about the past. Tomorrow was her future.

JARED LOOKED AROUND his backyard at the activity— Ellis setting up tables, Neal and a couple of his hands stringing lanterns in the trees. He shook his head. "We should have eloped."

"Too late," Shannon said, setting the box containing the new shoes she had bought to go with her dress on the front seat of his truck. The dress, in its clear plastic bag, was hanging from a hook over the passenger window. "Besides, Wynette has worked her heart out on this wedding. She would never forgive us."

"I don't see why you have to go to the Dickerson's to get dressed. I promise I won't peek."

She raised herself up on her toes and kissed him. "Humor me. I want to knock your socks off the first time you see me."

"Why stop at my socks?"

"After the reception, after everyone has gone home, then we'll discuss socks . . . and various other unnecessary articles of clothing."

He rolled his eyes. "You're killing me." Then on a more serious note, he asked, "Is Lily okay spending the night at the Dickerson's?"

"Are you kidding? She's already volunteered to get up and feed Josh his breakfast. And speaking of that, I better get over there before she drives Donna Jean nuts." She reached over to open the door of the truck, but he stopped her.

"Do you realize that the next time I kiss you, I'll be your husband?"

"I know," she whispered, her eyes misting. "Do you realize that this is the happiest day of my life?" She put a hand to his cheek and stroked it. "I love you so much, Jared."

"And I love you."

"Hey, Jared," Neal called out. "Just kiss her, and get your butt over here, or you're gonna be saying 'I do' in the dark."

"Keep your shirt on." He turned back for one more kiss, but she was already in the truck.

"See you in—" she checked her watch "—exactly three hours and twenty-two minutes," she promised, then blew him a kiss, and drove off.

LILY CAME RUNNING out of the Dickerson house the minute she saw the truck pull up. "Mama, Mama, you gotta come see the new kittens. Ellis said I could have one. Can I, Mama? Can I, please?"

"Whoa," Shannon said. "One major event at a time, sweetheart. Today, we marry Jared. Tomorrow we'll talk about cats."

"She's a single-minded little thing when she wants to be." Donna Jean stepped onto the porch, holding three-week-old Joshua in her arms.

"Tell me something I don't know." Shannon carried her dress and shoes, along with a small bag containing her makeup into the house.

Growing up with brothers, Shannon had never realized what a difference women friends could make in her life. Oh, she'd had school friends, but no one close. She had married Hal her first year in college, and the wives of his buddies formed her circle of friends. But she had never related to them the way she did to Wynette and Donna Jean. Most of those women had marriages similar to her own, and looking back, they were more like fellow victims than real friends. It was pure pleasure to share the hours before her wedding with true friends.

Wynette, Ellis and Neal had arrived, cleaned up and dressed up, and now they, along with Lily and Donna Jean, were ready to drive to Jared's place. Neal was chauffeuring today, and in charge of coming back for Shannon.

"Sure you don't mind being here by yourself while Neal takes us over?" Wynette asked. "I could stay, and ride with you."

"No, really. It would be kind of nice to have a few minutes alone."

"All right then, we better get goin'. Neal will be back in a jiffy."

Shannon kissed Lily goodbye, then waved them off, and went back into the bedroom where she had dressed. Standing in front of a full-length mirror, she admired her wedding dress.

True, it wasn't the fancy white gown every girl dreamed of, but then she wasn't a girl anymore. She was a woman, with a woman's dreams. The dress she had selected, with Donna Jean's help, was simple, elegant and made the most of her figure. It buttoned down the front all the way to the hemline which almost reached her ankles. A princess style made of shimmering beige silk with a scalloped neckline and long, fitted sleeves, the dress flowed around her with each step. It was understated, and maybe even a bit old-fashioned, but the moment Shannon spotted it in a shop in Fort Stockton, she knew it was the one. She'd decided to forgo a veil, and had done her hair swept up and captured at her crown, then strategically placed some fresh flowers among the curls.

She smiled back at her reflection. If she did say so herself, Jared's socks were definitely about to be knocked off. The sound of tires crunching on the gravel driveway told her Neal was back to collect her. With one last glance in the mirror she went into the living room.

"You were gone so long I thought you had forgotten about me," Shannon said, her back to the front door as she lifted the florist box containing her delicate bridal bouquet of roses and baby's breath. She turned, expecting to find a smiling friend…and froze. The box tumbled from her nerveless fingers and hit the floor.

"Hello, darlin'," said the dark, curly-haired man standing in the doorway. "Long time no see."

10

SHANNON SHOOK her head in disbelief even as she spoke his name. "H-Hal."

"In the flesh. You're looking good, Shannon. Real good, in fact." He glanced around. "Where's the kid?"

"G-gone. She's...she's not here," she said, numb with shock.

He shrugged. "We can always get her when we're ready to leave."

"Leave?"

"Sure. I've come all this way to bring you back to West Virginia where you belong."

Shannon stared at him as if he had lost his mind, then realized that he had. At least on some level, because in his twisted brain he had never gotten past thinking of her as his wife, his property. She realized with chilling certainty that he never would.

If she had any hope of reasoning with him, it went right out the window. Her only hope was escape, and in order to escape she had to come up with a plan. But for any plan to work, Shannon knew she had to keep Hal from raging. No matter what it took.

"Shannon? Did you hear me?"

"Y-yes." Now that the initial shock of seeing him had worn off, her mind whirled, calculating a method of escape. She was no match for his brute strength, but if she could get away from him, she could hide until Neal arrived. She looked around the room for something she could use as a weapon to defend herself, and spied a lamp base on an end table about ten feet away. It looked substantial enough for her purposes, and she began backing toward it.

"Shannon—"

The sound of Neal's truck on the gravel driveway cut him off. "Don't you open your mouth, you hear me?"

She was a split second away from screaming Neal's name when Hal reached around behind him, and pulled out a gun.

In that instant everything changed. Hal had never carried a weapon before. The fact that he had one now was a sign that he was more unbalanced than ever, and it turned Shannon's blood to ice. Neal would be coming through the door any second, and she had to warn him.

Hal positioned himself so that when the door opened he would be behind it.

Dear Lord, no, she thought. The front door flung open.

"Hey, Shannon, who does that car—"

"Neal!"

In a blur of motion, Hal stepped out, raised the gun, and struck Neal on the back of his head. Neal crumpled to the floor.

"Oh, my God." Shannon rushed over to him. There was a bloody gash on the side of his head, but he was alive.

"Get away from him," Hal ordered, pointing the gun at Neal's bleeding head.

"But he's hurt."

"Get away from him. You didn't really think I was going to let you marry him, did you?"

"Mar— I'm not marrying him. This is Neal Hartly."

"You're lying. Look at him, all dressed up for your wedding."

"Hal, he's not the one. Look." She picked up Neal's left hand, and pointed to the plain gold band on his ring finger. "I'm telling you the truth."

"Hartly? Not, Markham?"

"No." She scrambled over to the sofa table, and snatched a handful of tissues. Think, think, she ordered her frenzied brain. She had to escape and she couldn't do it without a plan. One thing was in her favor. Hal might know Jared's name, but he obviously didn't know his face.

"Where is he?"

"Who?" she asked, feigning ignorance. Gently she dabbed at the blood around the gash in Neal's head.

"Don't play dumb with me, Shannon. Where is Markham?"

"He's . . ." If Hal knew Jared was only minutes away there was no telling what he might do. "He's waiting at the church."

As soon as the words were out of her mouth, Shannon knew she had her plan. It wasn't dynamic or even original, but if she was convincing enough, it would work. At least it would keep Hal away from Lily. And give Jared time to find her.

"Yeah? Well, he can wait 'til Hell freezes over."

"I doubt he'll wait that long, but it doesn't matter." Neal was out cold, and probably had a concussion, but she had managed to stop the bleeding.

"What do you mean, it doesn't matter?"

Shannon got to her feet. "I mean, that I had already decided not to marry Jared before you ever showed up. I couldn't go through with it."

Obviously, he hadn't expected this turn of events, and for a moment he just watched her. "Why not?" he finally asked.

She sighed. "Because I realized it was no good. It wouldn't work. I thought I could start a new life without you, but I was stupid—" she had to grit her teeth to get around the word "—to think you wouldn't find me. You always do."

"And you always run."

"Not anymore. I'm tired of running, Hal." She sat down in a nearby rocking chair. "And I never would have admitted it before, but trying to stay on the run with a child is enough to wear even the strongest woman down."

"But you were set to marry this Markham fella."

"I told you, I couldn't go through with it. Neal, the man you knocked out, was coming back to get me, and . . . and take me to Alpine. The, uh, couple that's taking care of Lily—this is their ranch—went to the church to . . . to tell Jared I wasn't coming. I was supposed to meet them later at the café."

"Then what?"

"They were going to drive us to the bus station."

"Where were you going?"

She shrugged. "One place is as good as the next. Sooner or later you would have found us."

"Damn straight I would have."

"I'm just so tired of being alone. Back home I had my brothers, my friends. But now . . . I had no idea how hard it would be."

"Big bad world out there, isn't it?"

Oh, he was gloating, loving every minute of her groveling. "Yes, but it's more than that, Hal." She lifted her eyes to his. It was go for broke time. "I realized I . . . I still had feelings for you."

He narrowed his gaze at her. "If you're trying to sweet-talk me, forget it."

"No, it's the truth. You were my first love, and I'll always feel something for you." *Contempt* was the word that came to mind. "Besides, I've finally come to understand that the only time we had trouble was when I disobeyed you. I'm so sorry." Shannon thought she might throw up from the bitter taste of her words.

"If you're so all-fired sorry, why didn't you just call and come home?"

"I was ashamed of the way I treated you. For all I knew, you had the cops looking for me."

"I should have."

"I'm grateful that you didn't. I wouldn't blame you if you didn't want anything to do with me."

Shannon sat quietly, submissively . . . praying as she had never prayed before. She watched the expression on his face and could tell he was trying to decide if he believed her or not.

"You're willing to go back with me? Just like that?"

"Just like that."

"I don't believe you."

"Would you believe me if I said I would marry you again?"

Shock flickered across his face for a moment. "How do I know you're not just stringing me along until you can run away?"

Shannon licked her lips, knowing this was her last roll of the dice. He would either believe her, or . . .

"The Mexican border is only sixty or seventy miles south of here."

"So?"

"So, there's no waiting period. We could get married today." Her stomach roiled at the thought, but she would even go through with it, if it would keep Lily and Jared safe from this demented man.

Then she played her trump card.

"And I'll leave Lily here. My friends—the ones that were going to drive me to the bus station—are crazy about her. I'm sure they wouldn't mind letting her stay with them for a few days. We could pick her up on our way home. I could call them—" She reached for the phone.

"Don't touch it!"

Meekly, Shannon folded her hands in her lap. "All right. Whatever you say."

"If this is some kind of trick, you'll be sorry, Shannon."

"I know." She held her breath, waiting.

Hal paced back and forth in front of her, stopped, studied her, then started pacing again. The whole time Shannon was trying to think of how she could leave some kind of sign or message so that Jared would know which direction they traveled.

"You'd go with me, and leave the kid behind?"

She looked him straight in the eyes. "For a few days." Please, God, she thought, let Jared find me in a few hours.

"Right now?"

"I won't even bother to change clothes."

Hal's gaze drilled her, searching for any sign of betrayal. Heaven must have heard her prayers because he put the safety back on the gun, and stuck it into the waistband of his jeans. Relief flooded Shannon's entire body.

"Let's go," he ordered.

"I've got to call my friends—"

"Dammit, I told you not to touch the damn phone!"

Shannon shrank back from the familiar prelude to rage. "I have—have to contact my friends."

"No."

"What if they think something has happened to me and call the police?"

He thought about that for a moment, then said, "Leave them a note, but make it short, and don't tell them where we're going. Say you'll call later."

Thank Heaven, she thought. She had no doubt Hal would read whatever she wrote, so it would have to be subtle. She tore a page from a notepad Wynette kept by the phone and wrote:

Dear Mack and Pit,

My ex-husband has come for me, and we've decided to try again. I would appreciate it if you could watch Lily for a couple of days. Maybe now she can go on that picnic Jay promised her. I'll call you tomorrow.

                                    Thanks for everything,
                                    Shannon

Hal snatched the paper from her the instant she finished writing.

"Mack and Pit? What kind of game are you—"

"It's no game. Honest, the husband's name is Mack, and his wife's name is Petunia. Everyone calls her Pit."

"What is this about a picnic?"

"One of their ranch hands promised to take Lily on a picnic with his kids, that's all."

He read the note again, then handed it back to her. "Put it where they'll see it, and let's get the hell out of here."

A half hour later Jared, followed by Ellis and Tucker Weiss, came through the door just as Neal was trying to get to his feet. Jared caught him under the arms when he staggered.

"Where's Shannon?" Jared wanted to know immediately.

"What happened?" Ellis asked.

"Somebody..." Neal touched the gash on his head "...came in the door...hit me from behind."

"Neal?" Jared was almost shaking the already dazed man. "Where is Shannon?"

Neal looked around, trying to focus. "Don't... know."

"She left a note."

Jared's head snapped up. Tucker was standing a few feet away, holding a note. "You better take a look at this. It doesn't make any sense to me but—"

Jared all but jerked the note from Tucker's grasp. "Dear, God," he whispered when he finished reading. "He's got her."

"Who?"

"Jackson. Shannon's ex-husband. He's been hounding her ever since their divorce."

"Then why would she go with him?"

"She wouldn't. And she would never leave Lily unless she was forced to. The main reason she answered my ad in that magazine was to get away from Jackson."

"Why would she address a note to a couple of dogs?" Tucker asked.

For the first time since realizing something was very wrong when Shannon was late to her own wedding, Jared smiled. "Because she knows that occasionally Mack and Pit help me track perpetrators. She's trying to tell us to track her."

"Okay, I'm with you so far. But what's this business about a picnic, and who the hell is Jay?"

Jared read the note again, then again before he realized what the cryptic message meant. "Not long ago I had to cancel a picnic, and I promised I would make it up to her. I'm Jay, and they're headed south."

"How can you be sure?"

"Because the canceled picnic was supposed to be along the El Camino del Rio. She wants us to know they've gone south."

"Toward the border," Tucker reminded him.

"You call it in," Jared said, peeling out of his suit jacket, discarding his tie. Tucker headed for the phone.

Jared went over to where Neal was nursing his injured head. Ellis had brought him some ice wrapped in a tea towel. "Neal, did you see the guy that hit you?"

"Nope. I stepped through the door, and the lights went out."

"Can you remember anything about what happened? Anything Shannon might have said, or anything you heard?"

"It all happened so fast, Jared. I wish I could be more help, but . . ."

"What?"

"There was a car here when I drove up. I remember thinking it was one I'd never seen before."

"What color?"

"Light blue, I think. No, gray. Yeah, gray."

"Can you remember a make or model?"

Neal made the mistake of shaking his head, and groaned. "Not sure. Ford, maybe. A sedan."

"Thanks," Jared said.

Tucker was already on the phone with the authorities, and relayed the information Neal had provided. "Got an APB out on the vehicle with a description of Shannon. If they're going south the first obstacle will be getting into the park. Rangers have been alerted. They'll contact us the minute there is a sighting."

"If you think I'm going to wait around for someone to spot them, you're crazy." Jared was already out the door.

"Hold on," Tucker called. "You okay here?" he asked Ellis and Neal. When Ellis assured him they were fine, Tucker took off after Jared, who already had his truck in reverse.

Tucker yanked open the door, and jumped in. "Take it easy, we'll get this guy. And Shannon's smart. She left that message, didn't she?"

Jared put the truck into gear and it roared out in a spray of gravel. "You don't understand, Tuck. This guy messed her up the last time he caught her. He's a rager, an abuser. If he goes off the deep end, she won't be able to defend herself."

Tucker strapped himself in. "He's not going to get past us and the park rangers. And he's not stupid enough to go cross-country."

Jared shot him a hard look. "The guy is one of those macho types. Into guns, and survival training. He probably fancies himself more than a match for the law."

Tucker began removing his tie. "Then I suggest you step on it. We need to get your dogs, and our weapons."

IT WAS NEARLY DUSK when Hal approached the entrance to Big Bend National Park. He handed Shannon a map.

"How much farther to the border?"

"Maybe another twenty miles to Boquillas," she lied.

"I hope to hell they've got a decent motel."

Shannon cringed. "I'm sure they will."

They were fifth in a line of cars waiting to enter the park.

"What's taking so long?" Hal put down his window, and stuck his head out. "Those aren't just rangers up there. They've got cops, too. They're making everybody get out, like they were..." He pulled his head back inside the truck. "Like they were looking for somebody." The glance he gave her was pure hatred, raw, primal. "You wrote something in that note, didn't you?"

Her eyes wide with fear, she shook her head,

"Yes, you did. It was all a setup."

Shannon knew what was coming but she wasn't quick enough to steel herself.

"You lying bitch," Hal yelled as his fist struck her jaw. Shannon saw stars, then nothing but blackness.

When she came to, her head felt as if it had been used as a kettle drum, her bottom lip was cut and bleeding, and her body was being whipped back and forth as the car bounced violently. She blinked, realizing they were no longer on a road, but headed cross-country. In the dark!

Behind the wheel, his mouth set in a hard line, Hal was punctuating each dip, roll and pitch of the car with an obscenity. They hit a hole or low spot, throwing Shannon hard against the door. Her head hit the window, and she groaned.

"Shut up," he growled.

She deliberately let her head loll to one side as if she were still unconscious, but opened her eyes slightly. If she could get a fix on a few landmarks, then she could find her way back when she found a chance to escape. *If* she found a chance to escape.

No, she couldn't afford that kind of thinking. Jared would find her. He would read the note, and know what she was trying to tell him. He would find her.

Suddenly the car jerked to a stop. Hal shoved the gearshift into park, killed the motor and pulled the keys out of the ignition. Still feigning unconsciousness, Shannon's head dropped back on the headrest, and she let her body go limp. Outside all she could see was the outline of a stand of trees some twenty or thirty yards away.

Hal popped the trunk lid, and got out of the car. Then she heard noises that sounded as if he were unloading something from the back. If she could get out of the car, and run into the trees . . . Before she could finish the thought her car door was flung open. Hal reached over, unbuckled her seat belt, and yanked her out of the car. He threw her to the ground.

"I ought to kill you right here and now. I would if I didn't think I might need you as a hostage to get out of this godforsaken country."

He kicked her in the ribs. "Get up. You've been playing possum for the last ten minutes."

Shannon groaned, the pain in her rib cage making her gasp for breath. He raised his foot to kick her again, and she opened her eyes.

"That's more like it. Now, I said, get up."

Slowly, she rolled on her side, and got to her knees. But it wasn't fast enough for him. He reached down, grabbed the cluster of curls atop her head, some still dotted with flowers and pulled her up by her hair.

"Don't give me more reason to kill you, Shannon. You're hanging by a thread as it is." He shoved her up against the car where he could keep an eye on her.

Now she saw what he had hauled out of the trunk. Equipment. Lots of it. A camouflage jacket, which he already had on. Night goggles. Two rifles, one with a scope, probably infrared. And plenty of ammunition.

"Where are we going?" she asked, holding the right side of her rib cage. Merciful heavens, but it hurt to breathe.

"Into those hills."

"In the dark? You're insane."

In a move so quick she didn't even see it coming, he reached up and captured her face in one hand, squeezing her jaw until she thought he might break it. "I won't tell you again to shut up."

When he released his hold, the rush of blood back into her face was almost painful. He was insane if he planned on trekking into the mountains at night. She had no idea where they were, but she surmised that he had panicked when he saw the police at the park entrance. For all she knew, they could be a mile from the road they had been on or ten miles from the border.

Busy stuffing equipment into a backpack, Hal straightened, listening.

Shannon's heart leapt. Was that the sound of a helicopter somewhere off to the right? Oh, please let it be.

"Put this on." Hal threw a plastic camouflage-colored poncho at her. "And start walking toward those trees," he ordered, slipping on the backpack. When she didn't move fast enough to suit him, he grabbed her arm and practically dragged her along with him. In seconds they were in the trees. Hal pushed her to the ground then hunkered down beside her. Overhead the *whop-whop-whop* of the helicopter became louder.

From their position Shannon could see the chopper had spotted the car. Hovering, it shined its intensely bright searchlights on the vehicle and surrounding area. Beams of light swept the stand of trees that provided their cover, then moved on. Finally, the helicopter moved away to search another area. They stayed where they were for several more minutes, then Hal yanked her to her feet.

"Move. Ahead of me." He fitted the night goggles to his face, and shouldered a rifle. "And don't even think about running. I'd catch you before you got twenty feet. And you wouldn't be happy when I caught you, Shannon. I promise."

"I can't see where I'm going."

"I can. Keep walking straight ahead."

Only once did she glance back, but she was almost certain she saw lights in the distance. Headlights, she wondered? Could that be Jared and other officers coming to rescue her? It was only a glimpse, but it was enough to bolster her sagging hopes.

Using the night goggles to direct her, Hal continued their forced march into the hills. The lower half of Shannon's once beautiful dress became shredded as the undergrowth clawed at the fabric like demons trying to hitch a ride. By the time they made it up into the rocky hills she was cold, dirty and exhausted. She had no idea how much time had passed. It felt like days.

Hal marched them up to the crest of a peak that was more rock formation than mountain. Even though he wasn't familiar with the lay of the land, he knew the kind of high place needed to provide a vantage point. From his position atop the plateau he could easily see anyone that approached.

He shoved her down between two huge boulders. "Stay there." Then he moved six or eight feet away, almost to the edge of the peak. He put his rifle down, pulled a small tripod out of his backpack, set it up, and snapped a night scope into place.

"Wh-what are you g-going to do?" Shannon asked, trying to keep her teeth from chattering.

"Wait for daylight, then get the hell out of here."

"You can't get away."

"Sure I can. I could live in these mountains for a week, and they would never find me."

"Then why don't you just go? Leave me here. You could be in Mexico in no time. I promise I won't tell—"

His harsh laughter cut her off. "You think I'll fall for that a second time? Oh, no, darlin'. We're going with your original plan. You and me, and a justice of the peace. Then I'm going to take you back."

She couldn't believe she heard him right. He couldn't mean he actually intended to marry her. "I won't . . ." She heard something. Another helicopter? She stood up. "I won't do it." This way, Shannon prayed. Come this way.

"Sure you will." Now, Hal had heard the sound. It was definitely a helicopter. "Get down."

"No." She whipped off the poncho as the sound of the helicopter blades became a roar. In the light of a waning moon what was left of her beige silk dress shone like a bright beacon. "You might as well kill me because I'm not going anywhere with you. Not now. Not ever."

As he turned to reach for his rifle, Shannon saw her chance, and ran for her life.

"Bitch!" he yelled, his voice almost drowned out as the helicopter came roaring over the tops of the trees, searchlights crisscrossing the face of the mountain.

Shannon heard the gunfire, and knew Hal must be shooting at the helicopter, but she didn't look back. Now that he had been spotted, she knew it was only a matter of time—perhaps even minutes—before officers would arrive. Picking her way in the dark through rocks and shrubs she stumbled, falling hard on her left knee. Sobbing with pain, she got up, took several steps, then stopped.

"Oh, God, no," she cried. She had run right to the edge of the plateau. Right to the edge of a sheer drop-off.

Then she heard someone running behind her. Hal! She had to hide.

Jared and a handful of other officers had worked their way up the back of the mountain, and around to the plateau. They came out of the trees just as Jackson started firing on the helicopter. Before they could return fire, Hal started running.

With his heart in his throat, Jared prayed Shannon was all right. But he didn't see her. What if Jackson had already... No, he couldn't, wouldn't think like that. With Tucker right behind him, he took off after Jackson.

But the chase was short-lived. In minutes Jared and the others had Jackson cornered with them in front of him, and an eighty-foot drop-off behind him. Not surprisingly, in the face of an armed helicopter and almost a dozen law enforcement officers, Jackson threw down his rifle.

"This one's mine," Jared said.

Tucker didn't argue. Jared moved in, his gun aimed at Jackson. "Spread your feet. Put your hands behind your head."

"Where is Shannon?" he demanded as Jackson assumed the position. Standing directly in front of Hal Jackson with less than three feet separating them, Jared fought the urge to smash the man's face in. "Where is—"

"Jared!"

From over Jackson's shoulder, Jared saw Shannon stand up from behind a rock. He only took his eyes off Hal for a split second, but it was enough. Jackson dropped and lunged all at the same time.

Shannon screamed as Hal knocked Jared to the ground, and jumped on top of him, fists swinging. The other officers converged on the scuffle, but before they could separate them, Jared and Hal rolled toward the ledge.

"Hey," one officer yelled. "They're going over."

But Tucker Weiss already had a hand on Jared's shirt, pulling him back. Hal wasn't so lucky. He slid off the edge of the plateau, falling only a few feet before grabbing hold of a tree growing between two rocks.

"Help me," Hal called frantically, his feet dangling some sixty-plus feet from the bottom of the mountain.

With an officer holding on to Tucker, and Tucker holding tight to him, Jared stretched out a hand. Hal grasped it with one hand, then with both. The officer pulled him up to solid ground.

Jared had barely let Jackson go and got to his feet before Shannon came flying into his arms. Holding on to each other tightly, it would have been difficult to say who was smothering whom with the most kisses.

girl had twenty-exclamations, and two to interest her.
To wake in the Dying and his arms blurring on it
sometimes a child would have been difficult to say

Epilogue

"I NOW PRONOUNCE YOU man and wife. What God has joined together, let no man put asunder." The minister smiled and gave the groom a nod. "You may kiss the bride."

Jared Markham was way ahead of him. Scooping his soon-to-be-adopted daughter up with one arm, he embraced his wife with the other, and kissed her deeply. The entire gathering of their friends applauded.

"Yippee!" Lily said, her little arms around Jared's neck. "Now we get to stay here forever and ever, don't we, Mama?"

"Forever and ever," Shannon repeated, smiling up at her new husband.

"'Bout time y'all got around to havin' a proper weddin'." Wynette gave Shannon a big hug while Ellis pumped Jared's hand.

"Now, Mama," Donna Jean said, holding three-month-old Josh propped on her hip. "You know, they wanted to be done with their trip to West Virginia and all that legal stuff before throwing this party. Besides, it's not like they've been living in sin for the last three months."

"Oh, it's absolutely, one hundred percent legal." Jared sat Lily down, then slipped his arms around his wife.

Wynette put a hand on her hip. "Goin' off to a justice of the peace in the middle of the night. That's the kinda stuff teenagers do."

"I wasn't taking any chances." Jared kissed Shannon's temple. "I came too close to losing her. The minute we got down off that mountain, I found a justice of the peace and made it legal."

Shannon leaned back in her husband's arms, and gazed up at him. "As if I would want it any other way."

"I'm going to hold you to that for say, the next fifty or sixty years."

"I had more like forever in mind."

"Even better," Jared said as he kissed her again.

Realizing when three-plus was definitely a crowd, Wynette nudged Ellis. Donna Jean nodded, taking Lily's hand to lead her over to the refreshments. "Don't get so carried away you forget to cut the cake," Neal called over his shoulder.

Jared waved him on. "I suppose we will have to join our guests."

"Hmm. I suppose," she said, luxuriating in the feel of his arms around her.

"The sooner they eat, the sooner they'll all go home," he reminded her.

"And the sooner we'll be alone."

"Works for me."

She smiled. "Then we can start our second honeymoon."

"We never really had a first." Jared turned her to face him. "I'm sorry about that. I wish we could have gone—"

Her fingers against his lips stopped him. "I don't need a honeymoon. I don't need anything but you and Lily and our life together." She lifted her hand, admiring the ring guards that had been added a few moments ago to the plain gold band Jared had given her at their first ceremony. He had taken the agates and opals they had found that day at the Woodward Ranch, and had the ring guards custom-made. They were stunning, and special. Like her life.

"You know, I still can't figure out how I got so lucky." Smiling, he shook his head. "That silly ad. The odds were at least a million to one against me. Yet here you are."

"Never call that ad silly. And if anyone is lucky, it's me. I don't know what might have happened if you hadn't understood my note, and come after me that night. It makes my blood run cold just to think about it."

"All of that is in the past now. Jackson is going to be a guest of the Texas Department of Corrections for a lot of years. And after Texas is done with him, he's got some charges to face in West Virginia." He held her tighter. "You're safe and so is Lily. No more running. No more secrets."

"No more secrets," she whispered against his lips.

Well, maybe one more. A sweet, tiny secret she would share with him tonight when they lay in each other's arms. And they would dream about a son. And one day she would tell their son as she now told their daughter, the story of how the little princess and her mother had gone looking for a hero and found love, and a family. And happily ever after.

'Twas the Night Before Christmas...

And all through the inn, not a creature was stirring....
Except college prof Eve Vaughn and the gorgeous, sexy
stranger she'd met. They were sharing the most passionate
night of their lives. It didn't matter that they'd go their
separate ways on Christmas morn. Little did Eve know
madly-in-love Max had *no* intention of letting his special
gift escape!

Enjoy #614 CHRISTMAS WITH EVE by Elda Minger,
available in December 1996.

Five sensuous stories from Temptation about heroes and
heroines who share a single sizzling night of love.... And
damn the consequences!

MEN OF WHISKEY RIVER

Three sexy, unforgettable men
Three beautiful and *unusual* women

Come to Whiskey River, Arizona, a place "where anything can happen. And often does," says bestselling author JoAnn Ross of her new Temptation miniseries. "I envision Whiskey River as a romantic, magical place. A town like Brigadoon, hidden in the mists, just waiting to be discovered."

Enjoy three very *magical* romances.

> #605 *Untamed* (Oct.)
>
> #609 *Wanted!* (Nov.)
>
> #613 *Ambushed* (Dec.)

Come and be spellbound

Mail Order Men—Satisfaction Guaranteed!

Texas Man #5—*Trent Creighton*

This dedicated bachelor is at his wits' end. His three
matchmaking uncles want him to have a woman for
Christmas—and will do anything to see that he gets one!

Rusty Romero can't believe it—her grandmother
actually answered a personal ad for her. What is she?
Desperate? Not that her grandmother has bad taste.
Even Rusty has to admit Trent is drop-dead gorgeous.
But his ideas about women are right out of the Stone
Age. Trent needs a quick lesson in women's lib—and
Rusty knows she's just the woman to give him one.

#616 CHRISTMAS MALE
by Heather MacAllister

Available in December wherever
Harlequin books are sold.

#615 CHRISTMAS KNIGHT
by Lyn Ellis

Meet Nick De Salvo. Ex-cop. Full-time rebel. To save a friend, he took the rap for something he didn't do. Now he's lost his job, but not his instincts. And intuition tells him that someone wants to see him brought down. Unfortunately, his only suspect is T.J. Amberley—the woman who's stolen his heart....

All men are not created equal. Some are rough around the edges. Tough-minded but tenderhearted. Incredibly sexy. The tempting fulfillment of every woman's fantasy.

When it's time to fight for what they believe in, to win that special woman, our Rebels & Rogues are heroes at heart.

**Watch for CHRISTMAS KNIGHT
in December 1996, wherever
Harlequin books are sold.**

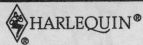

Merry Christmas, Baby!

A romantic collection filled with the magic of Christmas and the joy of children.

SUSAN WIGGS, Karen Young and
Bobby Hutchinson bring you Christmas wishes,
weddings and romance, in a charming
trio of stories that will warm up your
holiday season.

MERRY CHRISTMAS, BABY! also contains
Harlequin's special gift to you—a set of
FREE GIFT TAGS included in every book.

Brighten up your holiday season with
MERRY CHRISTMAS, BABY!

Available in November at
your favorite retail store.

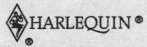

HARLEQUIN ®
®

Look us up on-line at: http://www.romance.net   MCB

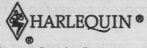